fromwhere
i Stand

Also by Tabitha Suzuma:

A Note of Madness

fromwhere i Stand

tabithasuzuma

The Bodley Head
London

FROM WHERE I STAND
A BODLEY HEAD BOOK 978 0 370 32906 2

Published in Great Britain by The Bodley Head,
an imprint of Random House Children's Books

This edition published 2007

1 3 5 7 9 10 8 6 4 2

The Random House Group Limited makes every effort to ensure that the
papers used in its books are made from trees that have been leaglly sourced
from well-managed and credibly certified forests.
Our paper procurement policy can be found at:
www.randomhouse.co.uk/paper.htm

Set in 11/18pt Baskerville by
Falcon Oast Graphic Art Ltd.

RANDOM HOUSE CHILDREN'S BOOKS
61–63 Uxbridge Road, London W5 5SA
A division of The Random House Group Ltd

Addressess for Random House Group Ltd companies outside the UK
can be found at: www.randomhouse.co.uk

THE RANDOM HOUSE GROUP Limited Reg. No. 954009
www.kidsatrandomhouse.co.uk

A CIP catalogue record for this book is available from the British Library.

Printed and bound in Great Britain by
Mackays of Chatham plc, Chatham, Kent

For Tansy

Acknowledgements

My deepest thanks go to: Tansy Suzuma for those plot discussions that crept into the night, my mother for all her help and encouragement, Akiko Hart for the confidence boost when I needed it most, Linda Davis for her support and advice, Sophie Nelson for her crucial attention to detail, and last, but by no means least, Charlie Sheppard for being such a wonderful editor and friend.

Chapter One

Raven stood at the window, waiting for the car. Three double-decker buses rumbled down the street, nose to tail, and joined the queue of traffic waiting at the lights. A cyclist pedalled furiously down the empty lane in the opposite direction. Somewhere the wail of a siren briefly rose and then faded. Over the bridge, the long queue of cars blurred into red pinpoints of light. A handful of raindrops suddenly splattered the windowpane. Night was falling and he could begin to see his blurred reflection in the glass. The cars in the street below were visible through his jean jacket but the white collar of his T-shirt stood out more strongly. His dark brown hair had lost the slicked-back look he had perfected that morning and now hung in his eyes. His face stared back at him, pale, serious. He narrowed his eyes to disguise a fleeting look of anxiety and dug his hands into his pockets.

'She's probably got held up in the traffic!' Sue burst out of the swing doors at the end of the corridor carrying a large tray, heavy with cutlery, and waddled past him down to the dining hall. There was a crash as she put the tray down on one of the long tables and a familiar clatter as she began to set the tables for supper. 'At this rate, Dave will be back with the others and you'll be having supper here.'

A red Micra suddenly swung into view at the end of the road, indicated left and began to pull up through the wet spray of puddles at the kerb. Raven stepped back from the window.

Sue came up behind him, wiping her hands on her apron, looking down into the darkening street.

'Here we go then! Are you sure you've got everything? Did you check under your bed?'

Raven nodded and hoisted the large rucksack over his shoulder. He reached for his suitcase but Sue got to it first and led the way downstairs.

Outside Joyce was stepping out onto the damp pavement, leaving the car door open and going round to unlock the boot. She said hello to Raven, took the suitcase and hoisted it inside, complaining to Sue about the rain and the traffic. Raven let the rucksack fall from his shoulder onto the suitcase. He slammed the boot shut and walked round to the passenger door.

'Hey!' Sue leaped after him and grabbed his arm. 'You weren't going to leave without a goodbye hug, were you?' She suddenly pulled him close so that his nose and mouth were pressed against her jumper, and for a moment he couldn't breathe. Then she released him back into the damp evening air.

He felt for the door handle. 'Bye,' he said.

'Now don't forget to send us a postcard, and remember to come back and see us from time to time!'

Raven nodded. He knew he would never go back and he doubted he would see Sue or any of the staff or kids at Bedford House ever again.

He drew the seat belt across him as Joyce flicked on the indicator and pulled out into the road. 'Got everything?' She turned her head and gave him a quick smile as he fumbled with the faulty catch. When he finally got it to click, he sat back and stared straight ahead.

'Excited?' Joyce turned to him with a smile again as she stopped at a zebra crossing. A woman hurried a little girl with a bright pink umbrella across the road. As they moved on, the lights from the streetlamps and the on-coming traffic caught in the rain-speckled windscreen, tracing a pattern of orange dots and circles over his jeans.

As Joyce drove smoothly through the rain-slicked streets, going against the traffic, Raven turned his head away and rested his elbow on the ledge below the window, chewing his thumbnail and gazing through the glass at the dark buildings whipping past. He felt cold suddenly.

'How was the trip today?' Joyce persisted in trying to make conversation.

Raven waited, drawing out the silence between them as long as he dared. 'OK,' he replied, without turning his head.

'The Russells are really excited about having you, you know.'

He said nothing.

'They must be wondering where you are. I told them I'd have you there by four.'

More silence.

'Anyway, nearly there now.'

They pulled off the main road into the quiet residential streets of Richmond and Raven began to feel his heart thumping in his chest. Joyce craned her head over the steering wheel, searching for a place to park. She stopped sharply and backed the car into a small space, hitting the kerb with a bump.

Raven got out and went round to open the boot. A

light popped on in a doorway three houses down and a man's voice called out, 'Hi there, you're here at last!'

'Yes – so sorry, the traffic on my way to pick him up was awful!'

'Can you stop for a cup of tea?'

'That's very kind but I really should get back. Oh, hi, Jackie! Sorry we're late.'

'Whoa!' Dan put out his hand as Raven stumbled backwards, dragging the suitcase from the boot. 'Here, I'll take that . . .'

Raven relinquished the suitcase but kept a firm grip on the strap of his rucksack.

'Nice to see you again, old pal.' Dan held out his hand and Raven accepted the handshake without looking up. He was even taller than Raven remembered, with a booming voice to match.

'Hello, Raven!' Jackie hurried round to the back of the car and patted him on the shoulder. Her short fair hair was pulled back from her eyes with a hairband, and she wore an exaggerated smile, her pink face eager.

Joyce slammed the boot shut. 'Right, well, I'll be off. You've got my number, so any problems, don't hesitate.'

'Thanks, Joyce,' Jackie said.

'Bye, Raven.'

'Bye.' He made his way towards the lit porch without looking back.

Inside the narrow hallway there was a sudden moment of confusion. Raven stopped short, unsure where to go next. Jackie bumped into him. Raven half turned but his rucksack caught on something hanging on the wall, sending it to the floor with a crash. He froze, eyes wide, and Dan broke the silence with a laugh. 'OK, bags down. I'll bring them up in a minute. Jackie, why don't you show Raven his room?'

Jackie squeezed past, exchanging looks with her husband before leading the way up the worn staircase. Raven lowered his rucksack to the ground and followed obediently. At the end of a short corridor on the first floor Jackie opened the door to a large square room, with white walls and a blue carpet. There was a computer on the desk and a decent-sized bed, not like those narrow bunks they'd had to sleep on at Bedford House. There was a wide bay window and a long mirror on one of the walls. 'You can put up posters or whatever you like,' Jackie said quickly, pointing to the packet of Blu-tak on the desk, 'and once we get you some books and things it will feel more like home.'

Raven looked at the large stretch of freshly vacuumed carpet, the Ikea furniture and the matching curtains and bedspread. It would never feel like home.

Dan lumbered in behind them with the suitcase and rucksack. 'So, what d'you think, Raven? Probably the last time we'll see it this tidy, hey?'

There was a silence. Raven looked at his bags set in the middle of the carpet, dwarfed by the size of the room. 'Shall I unpack now?' he asked.

'No hurry. Come and we'll show you the rest of the house . . . Little Miss lives here,' Dan said, pointing at a door covered in stickers. 'And I think this is meant to be a NO ENTRY sign so we'd better respect that for the moment, though I'm sure she'll take great delight in showing you round her pad herself . . . And here we've got the bathroom . . . And then just one more flight of stairs . . .' As he led the way, he reached back to take Jackie's hand in his.

'The master bedroom, messiest damn room in the house! Basically because I'm a slob and Jackie refuses to clear up after me, quite rightly. So now you've seen this, I won't have a leg to stand on when it comes to me telling you to pick your clothes up off the floor.'

The double bed was rumpled; books, CDs and huge piles of typed paper were stacked up against the walls. Several expensive-looking cameras and a tripod took up one corner and there were photos in every available space – some in actual frames, others in piles, or tacked to the wall. Photos of Dan and photos of Jackie, photos of Dan and Jackie together. Holiday snaps, bright white light and dashes of blue sea and sky. A little girl in a pink swimsuit clutching a rubber ring round her middle, blue eyes squinting up at the sun. The same little girl, older, wearing a flowery dress, sitting on Jackie's knee. All three of them at the edge of the sea, the little girl perched on Dan's shoulders . . .

There was a silence. 'Let's go down and meet the munchkin,' Dan said.

The kitchen and living room were merged together into one long living space, and at a large, chipped oak table the little girl from the photos sat swinging her legs, doing something messy with paints and pieces of sponge. She had grown since the holiday photos and her blonde hair was now cut into a short bob, a pink flower clip holding back a bunch of hair.

'Hello,' she said in a gravelly voice, looking up from her painting with a serious expression. 'My name's Ella.'

Jackie laughed her approval as if it were all part of a show. 'Good girl,' she said. 'Are you going to tell Raven how old you are?'

'Five and three quarters. My birthday's on the tenth of May. When's yours?'

'October,' Raven said.

'Same as Halloween's.'

Dan and Jackie laughed together. 'Raven's fourteen,' Jackie said. 'So, how many years older than you?'

'Nine,' Ella replied without missing a beat.

'Clever Ella Bella.' Dan came round to tickle her ribs, making her squirm and giggle. 'Now how about we put this beautiful artwork out to dry and start laying the table for dinner? Have a seat, Raven.'

Raven sat on one of the wooden chairs and watched the well-oiled family meal routine unfold before him. Dan seemed to be in charge of the food, stirring something sizzling in a large frying pan on the stove; Jackie carefully transferred Ella's soggy pictures to the sideboard and Ella fetched a dripping sponge and began to mop the table.

'A bit too much water there, pipsqueak.' Jackie took the sponge off her and went to squeeze it over the sink. 'Here we go, try again.'

Raven watched Ella wipe the table imperiously, glancing up at him several times to check that she still had his attention. Jackie laid the table and Dan dished out the food onto large chipped plates and Ella poured water from the jug into the glasses, liberally splashing the table in the process. Then they sat down and picked up their knives and forks. 'Tuck in,' Dan said to Raven.

Raven felt very tired suddenly, and not in the least bit hungry. He started to move the food around on his plate.

'Raven's going to be starting at Ushton Comprehensive on Monday,' Jackie said to Ella, her eyes on Raven. 'That's the big red building right next to your school.'

Ella levelled her serious gaze to his. 'That's the big boys and girls' school. What class are you going to be in?'

'Year Nine.'

'I'm in Year One,' Ella announced importantly. 'My teacher's called Miss Mann. She's nice. On Fridays she lets us have Choosing Time. Next year I'm going to be in Year Two. I'm the second cleverest in the class. Michael's the cleverest.'

'But remember we don't talk about who's the cleverest or the second cleverest,' Jackie said quickly. 'The only important thing is that you try your best.'

'I do try my best and that's why I'm the second cleverest,' Ella said.

There was a little hole in the wall opposite. If Raven squinted slightly, the blue wallpaper looked like waves, lapping at the mouth of a cave.

'Are you not a big fan of pasta?' Dan asked.

Raven swivelled his gaze back to them, suddenly aware that there had been a long silence. The first mouthful was still at the end of his fork, quietly con-gealing. He ate it quickly.

'Next week you can come with me to Tesco's and pick out some of your favourite food,' Jackie said brightly.

'I like pasta, Daddy,' Ella put in.

'What kind of things do you like to eat?' Dan asked.

Raven shrugged.

'No favourite meals?' Jackie this time.

'No.'

'I like pizza best,' Ella said. 'And fish fingers is my second bestest. And chips is my third bestest. And pancakes is my fourth bestest. And my fifth bestest is—'

'Why don't we tell Raven about some of the things we like to do all together at the weekend?' Dan cut in.

'OK.' Ella turned to look at Raven. 'We go to the park and we go to the swimming pool and we go to the zoo and we go to Legoland and we go to Pizza Express and we go to the Science Museum—' She broke off to draw breath.

'Not all in one weekend, mind you!' Jackie laughed.

'Raven, what do you like to do in your spare time?' Dan asked.

There was a silence.

'Go to the zoo?' Ella suggested.

Raven shrugged. There was another silence. Then

Dan said something about going camping at Easter. Jackie wondered if they still had their old tent. Ella protested that she didn't want to sleep outside because an ant might crawl into her mouth. Jackie started clearing the plates. 'But Raven only had one mouthful!' Ella protested. 'Why doesn't *he* have to eat everything on his plate?'

After he had finished unpacking, the room looked much the same as before, apart from the picture frame he had placed on one of the empty shelves above the desk. His clothes fitted easily into the top drawer of the four-drawer chest and the wardrobe held his empty rucksack and suitcase. At the end of his bed there were two neatly folded yellow towels with embroidered flowers at the corner. He sat down on his bed and looked at them. There was a knock on the door. He glanced up. Nothing happened. Another knock.

'Yes?' he said tentatively.

The handle turned and Dan came in, followed by Jackie.

'Great, are you all unpacked?' Dan looked round the empty room.

'We can go into town next weekend and get you some posters to put up on the walls or – or something,' Jackie

suggested hesitantly. 'Do you have any favourite, um –
bands, or um – football teams?'

'No,' Raven said.

Dan sat down in the swivel chair and gave himself a
little spin. 'What about computer games? PlayStation?
Bet you've got some favourites there!'

Raven shrugged.

'Sorry, pal, we don't mean to give you the Spanish
Inquisition,' Dan said suddenly. 'We're just eager to get
to know you, and we're so excited you've come to stay.
But, hey, there's no need to rush things.'

'No, we've got all the time in the world,' Jackie agreed.
'Now, Raven, do you remember where everything is? Is
there anything you need?'

He was supposed to nod to the first question and
shake his head to the second. So he did neither.

Jackie glanced uncertainly back at Dan.

'Do you like board games?' Dan asked. 'We've got
Cluedo and Trivial Pursuit and Monopoly . . . Shall we all
have a game tonight?'

'Good idea!' Jackie said.

They both looked at Raven. He looked back.

'I tell you what.' Dan stood up. 'We'll go and set it up
in the kitchen and you come down and join us if you feel
like it, or come and watch TV, or stay up here and do

your own thing if you prefer. Up to you, buddy, OK?'

Raven nodded.

They finally left.

He listened to their lowered voices and their receding footsteps on the stairs. Then, when silence fell, he moved back on the bed so that he was sitting against the wall with his knees drawn up, surveying the room around him. With his eyes he searched the white walls, the pale blue curtains, the empty surfaces. Suddenly his gaze stopped and returned to the curtains. He got up from the bed and went over to them, drawing them apart, revealing a sharp reflection of himself and the room behind him against a backdrop of darkness. He switched off the light and returned to his sitting position on the bed. At first nothing, then gradually the night sky turned from black to slate. The outline of a tree began to form, and through its branches he could just make out pinpricks of light from a distant aeroplane as it penetrated a thin veil of cloud. Raven's eyes locked onto it, drawing him out, up and towards it and away from the night.

He was awoken by a shaft of yellow daylight slanting across his pillow. He sat up in bed, blinking sleepily at the neat, uncluttered room, the smooth stretch of carpet, unlittered with smelly trainers or crumpled clothes. There was no creaky bunk above him, no acrid smell wafting down from Tommy's wet mattress, no clattering of plates from the kitchen below. All he could hear was the twittering of birds.

He listened at his bedroom door before opening it and making his way quickly down the corridor, past Ella's room, her door left ajar, and into the bathroom. He had a fast shower, feeling as if he were trespassing, half expecting a knock on the door and a voice demanding who was there. Once he was dressed he sat back on his bed, reluctant to start the day. But the sun was already high in the sky and the sound of voices and the clatter of plates drifted up from the kitchen. The sooner he got started, the sooner it would be over, he reasoned. Maybe they would even let him stay in his room. He braced himself, opened the door and went slowly down the stairs, trying to make as much noise as possible in case they were discussing him. But as usual it was Ella doing all the talking.

'. . . and when we came back into class after break, me and Lucy, we told Miss Mann that the boys had been bothering us all break time. And Miss Mann said, "What were the boys doing?" And so I said, "The boys told us we had to kiss their hands." And Miss Mann said, "Sam, is that true?" And Sam said, "Yes," and then Miss Mann started *laughing*! Then she stopped laughing and told the boys off but her shoulders were still wobbling—'

'Morning, Raven!' Jackie exclaimed.

'Morning.' He hung in the doorway.

Dan jumped up and pulled out a chair. 'Come and sit down. What would you like for breakfast?'

Raven sat and glanced at the array of cereal boxes, croissants and loaves spread out over the table. He reached for the nearest packet of cereal and poured some into the bowl in front of him.

'Did you sleep well?' Jackie asked him, an anxious smile on her face.

He nodded, pouring the milk, wishing Ella would start yakking away again. But she just watched him stonily.

'Were you warm enough?' Dan wanted to know.

Another nod.

'It must have felt a bit disorientating waking up in a strange bed,' Jackie went on. 'I know I always feel a bit confused if I spend the night away from home. Did you wonder where you were when you woke up?'

'No,' Raven said.

'Oh, well, good, you must be getting used to us already!' She gave a small laugh.

Raven took a mouthful of soggy cornflakes and swallowed it with difficulty.

'We were thinking we might go for a walk in the park since it's such a sunny day,' Dan said. 'How does that sound?'

Raven lifted his gaze from his bowl and nodded, forcing a smile.

The car was an old Ford. He sat in the back with Ella, who drew her knees up under her chin, put her thumb in her mouth and watched him soberly. Dan drove, his broad, tanned hands loose on the wheel, head almost touching the roof. Jackie talked about the weather in an attempt to cover the silence. Raven turned his head, looking out of the window to escape Ella's penetrating stare.

In the park the air was crisp and cold. The sky was a bright, painful blue and the ground a canopy of russet leaves. Ella led at a gallop and Raven hung back, hands dug deep in the pockets of his jacket, crunching curled sandpaper leaves underfoot. Jackie and Dan walked ahead of him, fingers entwined.

'Mummy, Daddy, look!' Ella suddenly stopped, pointing at a herd of wild red deer surveying them warily from the opposite hillside. At the head of the herd, a stag twitched its ears and sniffed the air nervously. Raven stared at it. Its antlers were enormous, jutting out from its head like the branches of a dead tree. Its huge craggy crown was almost bigger than the animal itself.

'Marvellous, isn't he.' Dan was walking back towards him. Jackie and Ella had moved on. Raven tore his eyes away from the deer and started walking again. Dan fell into step beside him. 'They look so proud and strong,' he went on, 'but really they are quite shy, frightened animals.'

They walked for a while in silence. Jackie chased Ella in the distance.

'Must be daunting, coming to live with a new family,' Dan observed.

Raven said nothing.

'I've never had to do anything like that, so I can only guess how it feels. But I remember when I was about thirteen, I was hopeless at French at school and so my parents sent me away on a French exchange programme. I was bloody terrified, I can tell you, getting off the plane in this foreign country, being picked up by this strange couple and their horrid teenage son who rolled his eyes whenever I tried to say something in French . . . There was this bush in the garden which we were told not to touch because the berries on it were poisonous and I even considered eating one of them so that I would get ill and have to go home. God, that was the longest two weeks of my life.'

There was a silence.

'But it did finally come to an end.'

Raven felt Dan's eyes on him. He stared fixedly ahead.

'So, I can't imagine what this must be like.'

Raven looked down at the small puffs of white air coming out of his mouth. They appeared in time with his steps. In – one, two; out – one, two.

'If there's any way we can make it easier, Raven, any way at all . . .' Dan exhaled heavily. 'Jackie and I really want you to be happy here. But we're not perfect and sometimes we might need some tips . . . So if there's anything you need, or anything we're doing wrong, you must tell us and we'll really do our best to put it right . . .'

Raven felt Dan's eyes on him again.

'Do you understand what I'm trying to say?'

Raven nodded.

'Will you point us in the right direction?'

Raven nodded again.

Dan's hand was on his shoulder. 'OK then, buddy.'

Ella ran into the play area and over to the swings, demanding to be pushed. Jackie collapsed on a bench and looked back at Dan. 'Your turn!'

There was only one bench so Raven sat on the swing furthest away from Ella, pressing his cheek against the cold metal chain. Ella swung her legs furiously, clamouring to be pushed higher and higher. Dan obliged and with a few strong pushes had her almost matching the height of the iron pole from which the swings hung.

'Dan, be careful!' Jackie exclaimed.

Ella whooped with delight. Raven wondered what would happen if she fell off the swing at its highest point – would she plummet straight down onto the asphalt or would the momentum carry her over the bushes and the fence beyond? But Dan had stopped pushing her now; in fact he was lightly catching the back of the swing in response to Jackie's request, backing away once Ella was swinging at a more acceptable height.

Ella scraped her feet along the ground to slow herself, jumped off, half fell, but was already running towards the slide. She shot down it head first, and was then on the roundabout, pushing herself around with one foot until she gathered enough speed to be able to sit back and let it turn on its own, her scarf streaming out behind her. When it slowed, she jumped off but continued to spin around, holding out her arms and yelling, 'I'm dizzy, I'm dizzy, I'm dizzy,' finally falling in a dramatic heap at her mother's feet. Dan said something about making a move and Raven walked out of the play area ahead of them, back towards the car.

That afternoon Jackie gave him his school uniform. 'Try it on and see if it fits,' she said. 'Then, if it needs adjusting, I can do it now.' His previous school hadn't had a school uniform. The last time he had worn a tie had been at Mum's funeral. Granny Bess had tied it for him then. She was in a home now. The white shirt and navy blue blazer were OK; the grey trousers were a bit long.

'Don't worry, I can turn those up for you,' Jackie said. 'Gosh, you look smart. Dan, doesn't he look smart?'

'I've got a school uniform,' Ella put in. 'It's a burgundy blouse and a grey dress and my blazer's same like yours. Mummy, can I show Raven my uniform?'

'It's in the wash, Ella,' Jackie replied, bending over the sewing machine. 'Raven, if you give me the uniform back, I'll sew on some name tags.'

Raven went upstairs to change, returned the clothes to Jackie and went back to his room again. There was a knock on the door and Dan came in. 'Here's your arsenal,' he said, placing a new rucksack on the chair. 'Use it wisely.' He departed with a grin.

The rucksack was a school regulation one, dark blue with the school logo on the front. Picking it up, Raven discovered it wasn't empty. He unzipped it and inside found a block of lined paper, a file with coloured dividers, four exercise books and a pencil case. The case was one of those shaped like a book, with three zipped compartments containing felt-tips, colouring pencils, ordinary pencils, two rubbers, a biro of each colour, two ink pens, a packet of cartridges and a geometry set. There was also a large scientific calculator. In the front pocket of the rucksack he found a *South Park* wallet containing a house key on a football key ring, five pounds in change, a mobile phone and a piece of paper saying *Jackie and Dan Russell* followed by one landline and two mobile numbers. He put everything back inside the bag and shoved it out of sight behind the desk.

The day ground on. Jackie and Ella insisted on a board game. They played Monopoly. Raven bought nothing and kept forgetting to collect £200 each time he passed Go. The fourth time, Ella tapped the side of her head and stuck out her tongue until Dan told her sharply to stop it. After dinner the television went on and he was finally able to escape to his room.

He didn't bother turning on the light. He sat against the head of his bed, his eyes gently adjusting to the penumbra, staring out of the window at the lights from the opposite houses. After a while he became aware of his name being called, repeatedly and impatiently, and the bedroom door swung open.

'Why are you sitting there in the dark?' Ella leaned against the doorjamb, the tip of her finger in her mouth.

Raven eyed her warily. She was wearing a pink nightie and her hair was combed back, wet from her bath. 'What are you doing?'

'Nothing,' he said.

'What are all those scratches on your arms?'

He didn't reply.

'Mummy told me to come and say goodnight.'

He waited. But the goodnight didn't come.

'This used to be my playroom.' She pushed the door open further, skipped over to the swivel chair and sat down. She lay back in it, stretching out her legs so that the tips of her toes just touched the floor, and swung herself gently from side to side. 'Now it's your room,' she stated. 'Where were you living before you came here?'

'Hounslow,' Raven said.

She frowned for a moment. 'With who?'

He shrugged. 'Other kids.'

'Is it true that your mummy died?'

He looked at her. Through her. He could almost make out the desk behind.

'My mummy said that your mummy died and your

daddy couldn't look after you any more. Is that true?'

'I never knew my dad,' Raven said. He could definitely see the outline of the desk, its edge unbroken, travelling straight across her forehead.

She sat up, suddenly breaking his concentration. 'I'm going to bed now,' she announced.

He looked at her expectantly.

'Are you starting at your new school tomorrow?'

'Yeah.'

'Yay! I'll be able to see you at second play, after lunch. My playground is right next to your playground and there's a little gap in the railing where Lucy and me sometimes sneak through to say hello to the big girls. Will you come and say hello to me at the fence?'

'Yeah.'

She turned in the doorway with a frown, her index finger raised. 'OK, don't forget. You have to come to the gap in the fence at second play after lunch. OK?'

'Yeah.'

She skipped happily down the corridor, leaving his door ajar.

Chapter Two

He woke just after seven and sat up against the head-board, watching a pale, watery dawn stretch across the rooftops. He had the feeling he'd hardly slept and there was a sickish, heavy weight in his stomach. It seemed incredible that in the time it took for the sun to set again, he would have had to get through a whole school day: get washed, get dressed, have breakfast, talk to Jackie, Dan and Ella, get in the car, get out of the car, go into the school building, go into his new class, speak to his new teacher, sit in class, go out to break, speak to some of the other kids, have lunch, have another break, sit in class again, go home with Ella, talk to Jackie, Dan and Ella again, do some homework, have dinner . . . and only then perhaps manage to escape for the night. It seemed impossible, insurmountable, totally unfeasible, and yet just like the cold, white dawn spreading across the sky, he had absolutely no say in the matter. It was going to happen whether he liked it or not; he was going to have to get through it whether he wanted to or not – only something dramatic like drinking bleach would stop the school day from running its course. And even then, even if he ended up in hospital, it would only be a matter of time before he was well again and back at Jackie and Dan's, and before he knew it he would be sitting here once more, watching the dawn break and contemplating the ghastly inevitability of the school day.

He knew it was worse, waking early, having time to consider the ordeal ahead, than waking at the last minute and having to start the day without giving it another thought, but this time was precious too – time when he was still on his own, safe in bed, in his room with a firmly closed door between himself and the outside world. He wished there was some way of stalling it, some way of stopping it right now and keeping the hands of his alarm clock frozen at ten past seven, some way of keeping that damn second hand from ticking its ruthless path round and round the clock face, moving the hours on. Or else he wished there was a way of accelerating time, of being able to close his eyes and skip forward twelve hours to the evening, to that moment when he stepped through his bedroom door and shut the Russells, school and everything else behind him for another night. But the only way to reach that point was to get through the next twelve hours, somehow to keep going, one painful step at a time, keeping his eyes firmly fixed on the finishing line.

'Mummy, Daddy, I'm awake!' Ella's excited voice floated through the door, signalling the irreversible start of the day. The urge to get back under the covers, blot out the rising voices and the growing light, suddenly became overwhelming, but he knew that to do that would be to give in, to lose the brittle shell he had begun to form between himself and the outside world. If he melted back into the warmth and softness of the pillows, he would be unable to ever wrench himself away and they would have to drag him kicking and screaming from his bed. And he couldn't bear for that to happen again, not here. So instead he rose stiffly, his movements quick and jerky – made the bed, listened at his door, dashed into the bathroom, locked the door, pulled off his T-shirt and boxers, turned on the shower, struggled with the knobs to find the right temperature, soaped himself, rinsed himself, wrapped the towel round himself, brushed his teeth, dashed back to his room, dried himself, put on the scratchy, starchy school uniform, brushed his hair, and then stopped and stared at himself in the mirror.

So this is what they would see. A fourteen-year-old boy with a pale face and wide blue eyes and light brown hair that tended to fall in his eyes. In the school uniform he'd be bound to blend in – OK, people always stared when a new kid arrived, but at least he managed to look, well, fairly normal. There were no telltale signs. He wouldn't mention Bedford House, just in case anyone had ever heard of it. Better still, he would say that his family had moved house, had moved from Hounslow to Richmond, and claim that was why he'd had to change schools.

'Did you sleep OK?' Jackie and Dan were both looking at him somewhat anxiously this morning. Jackie especially seemed over-bright and slightly frazzled, probably because Joyce had told them of his past experiences with schools. 'I have to say I'm not usually a fan of school uniforms but you do look really smart in a shirt and tie.'

'How about something a little more substantial for your first day?' Dan called over from the stove. 'I'm making bacon and eggs for Ella and me. Want some?'

Raven shook his head quickly and poured cereal into his bowl.

'Toast?' Jackie tried.

Again he shook his head.

Jackie took a bite of her own breakfast, then got up to brush Ella's hair. Ella swung her legs and munched on her toast, looking somehow older in her burgundy blouse and grey pinafore. Jackie fastened a red clip in Ella's hair and scrutinized her carefully. Dan shovelled a pile of bacon and eggs unceremoniously onto Ella's plate.

'Dan, that's too much!' Jackie instantly exclaimed.

'She's a growing girl, let her eat as much as she can!'

'Ella, let Mummy have some—'

'No, I want it, Daddy made it for me!'

Raven watched their antics, munching slowly, every so often taking another mouthful of tasteless, soggy cereal and forcing it down. More offers of food came his way and he rejected them mechanically, and eventually Ella grew tired of her breakfast, and Jackie started hunting for Ella's blazer and the car keys, and Dan said he was late for work, and Jackie shouted at Ella, and Ella went into a sulk, and Dan gave Ella three kisses, and then he gave Jackie one, and then he squeezed Raven's shoulder and said, 'Good luck, OK?' and then he was gone, and then they were getting into the car, and then Jackie was running back to the house to pick up Ella's blazer, and then they were driving with Jackie saying 'Shit' every time they had to stop at a red light.

The moment Ella flung off her seat belt and jumped

out of the car, Raven was greeted by that sickening familiar sound – the sound of children. Yelling, laughing, chatting, it all bled together into this kind of muffled scream. They dropped Ella off at the gate to her school and, after more hugs and kisses, she ran off with three other girls amidst cries of 'Look what I've got, look what I've got!' Jackie put her hand on Raven's shoulder to steer him towards the adjoining red-brick school, where pupils stood around in the playground in small groups (mainly the girls) or ran around after balls (mainly the boys). All the boys were dressed just like he was, but some of them had taken off their blazers and slung them over their shoulders, or hung them from the goalposts, or thrown them down on the ground over their school bags. Some of the boys were huge, over six foot tall, recognizable only as pupils by their school uniforms. Some were barely half their height, with blazers several sizes too big. Raven followed Jackie as she nervously traced a path between the flying balls, running boys and clusters of pupils, across the playground and in through the wide, double-doored mouth of the school building.

Inside was big. Big doors, long corridors, wide stairs, all white and scrubbed, but quieter.

'The headmaster's office is on the third floor,' Jackie said in hushed tones, as if fearing she would be overheard as they climbed the stairs. 'His name is Mr Miller. The deputy's office is next door – she's very nice, I've had her on the phone a few times – Mrs Briggs. You should go to her if you've got any problems, she's very approachable.' On the third floor Jackie stopped suddenly, a panicked look on her face. 'Have I got it right? Oh yes, it *is* here! Here we go . . .' She led him down a long corridor, the relief in her voice clear, and knocked on a door.

The headmaster introduced himself. He shook Jackie's hand and then Raven's, and after a quick exchange Jackie left, patting Raven on the shoulder and saying, 'I'll see you at three thirty, OK? I'll be at the gate.'

Raven nodded and followed the headmaster down the corridor.

'You're going to be in Nine H,' Mr Miller said, leading Raven up another flight of stairs. 'Your form teacher is Mrs Harrison. On the whole they're a good, hard-working class. So keep to the school rules and put your best foot forward and you should get along fine.'

He stopped outside a door, knocked and strode in. Raven heard a sudden silence, followed by a loud scraping of chairs.

'Thank you. Sit down,' the headmaster said. 'Mrs Harrison, I've brought you your new pupil.'

A large room, tall windows, a sea of white shirts, red ties and blank faces. A teacher standing by a whiteboard, pen in hand, looking past him at the headmaster. 'Thank you, Mr Miller.'

The headmaster left, the door closed. A collective mumble began to rise. 'Welcome to Ushton,' Mrs Harrison was saying. 'I'm Mrs Harrison and this is your form room. Now, where shall we put you . . . ? I need someone responsible to look after Raven as he's new to this school,' she announced, raising her voice to the rest of the class. 'Would somebody like to volunteer to be his buddy for the day?'

There was a hush, sideways glances and then muffled giggles. Raven felt his face burn.

'Come on, Nine H, there must be at least *one* responsible person in this class.'

Slowly a boy with a bleached-blond mohican sitting at the back raised his arm. There were exclamations of surprise and then nervous laughter. The boy sitting next to him laughed the loudest.

'No, I don't think you're a very good candidate, Kyle Jones.' More laughter. 'Anyone else?'

Nothing happened. More titters. Then a girl with long, messy blonde hair that hung in her eyes suddenly raised her arm, to the sound of wolf-whistles and jeering.

'*Thank* you, Lotte.' Mrs Harrison raised her voice over the noise. 'Alice, come and sit over here. Raven, you go next to Lotte. Right, right! Settle down! I don't remember giving anyone permission to start chatting!'

Raven walked blindly to his newly vacated seat. He put his bag on the floor and sat down. The teacher tapped loudly on the board and people's eyes began to swivel back to the front.

'OK, back to the questions. *I said, back to the questions, Kyle and Brett!* Raven, this is English and we're doing a comprehension on *To Kill a Mockingbird*. Daniel, can you pass Raven a copy of the book, please, and . . . wait, I've got it somewhere . . . a copy of the timetable? Right, now, where were we? Kyle, if I have to say your name once more you can go and see Mr Miller. Jennifer, read question three.'

A battered paperback and a copy of the timetable landed with a thud on Raven's desk. He glanced quickly at the book on the desk next to his and opened his book to the same page. Someone hesitantly read out a question.

'Hi, I'm Lotte,' the girl beside him whispered suddenly. 'I wasn't trying to embarrass you I just couldn't bear to see you having to stand up there like an idiot.'

Raven mumbled something in return and quickly turned away.

Gradually, as the sidelong glances and muffled whis-
pers began to die down and the pupils appeared to tire
of looking at him, Raven became aware of the frantic
beating of his heart. He stared down at his book and
watched the typeface jump and swim like ants running
around the page. He could feel the cold sweat slowly
congealing on his back and hear the sound of his rapid,
shallow breathing. He was aware of the arm of his
neighbour, stretched out carelessly along the side of her
desk, her shirt cuff undone, her skin very white, chipped
purple nail polish on her fingers. When the awful shriek
of the bell went, there was an immediate rising of voices
and scraping of chairs. 'Chapter Five for tomorrow!' Mrs
Harrison called out above the din.

Raven glanced around. Taking his cue from the
people about him, he stuffed the book and timetable in
his bag and stood up.

'It's bloody maths now,' Lotte mumbled, looking fed
up. 'Last door on the right. So where are you from,
anyway?'

'Hounslow,' Raven muttered in reply.

'You've just moved house?'

'Yeah.' That was easy.

He hung back as she gathered her stuff together and
made for the door, then waited until she had left the

classroom before going out into the hallway. Doors on either side were flying open as the corridors filled with pupils. When he got to the next room, he quickly took a seat at the back. He saw Lotte sit down beside the window and yawn as her friend joined her.

The boy who had first put up his hand took a seat next to Raven and motioned for his friend to come over and join them.

'Hi, I'm Kyle,' he said with a chipped-tooth grin. Raven noticed that he wore tiny gold studs in his ears; his hair was dyed so blond, it was almost white. 'This is Brett.'

'Hi,' Brett said. He was taller than Kyle, and beefier too, with a pale face, freckles and a short fuzz of red hair. 'What did you say your name was again?'

Raven felt his cheeks burn. 'Raven,' he said.

'Raving?' Brett said with a frown.

Kyle guffawed and tried to rap Brett on the head. 'No, you dumb-ass, he said *Raven*! Like the bird – you know – a raven.'

'Oh, *Raven*! You named after a bird?'

'Not just any bird – a blackbird,' Kyle said.

'So why didn't they just call you Blackbird?'

Kyle rolled his eyes and tapped the side of his head. 'Because that sounds stupid, *stupid*!' He leaned forward over Raven's desk. 'Sorry about my friend,' he said. 'He can be a bit thick sometimes.'

'Hey!' Brett gave him a playful whack, but was still laughing.

'What's all this racket? Right, in your seats! Maths books out! Kyle and Brett, how many times have I told you I do *not* want you sitting together?'

'Oh, sir! But we was being helpful. Look, we got a new boy in the class. His name is—' Kyle glanced at Brett.

'Raving,' Brett said. Laughter. Kyle didn't correct him. The maths teacher looked expectantly at Raven.

'Raven,' Raven said. It was hard to talk.

'But I thought he said *Raving*, sir,' Brett called out.

'OK, Brett, settle down.' The teacher glanced down at the register in his hand. 'You must be the new boy, Raven Win—'

'Winter,' Raven said. 'My name is Raven Winter.'

'Oh, right.' The teacher scribbled something in the register. 'Good, well, I'm Mr Rumbold, this is Year Nine double maths and this week we're doing fractions. Now, everyone open your books at page ninety-three.'

Raven didn't move. 'Here, you can share with me,' Kyle whispered, sliding his book across the gap between their desks. 'Don't worry about Brett, he always makes fun of people, especially people with weird names.'

At lunch time, as Raven inched his way down the packed staircase towards the canteen, he was suddenly aware of Lotte, pushing her way towards him.

'Hi,' she said breathlessly on reaching him.

'Hi,' Raven replied, eyes fixed on the slowly moving mass of bodies ahead.

'I just thought I should warn you – Kyle and Brett are fuckwits, so it's not a good idea to get too pally with them. They tend to rake certain kids in, have a bit of fun with them, then chew them up and spit them out again.'

Raven said nothing.

'Obviously it's up to you who you hang around with, but I just wanted to warn you. Kyle especially. He may seem all friendly and shit, but really he'll—' A couple of boys pushed between them and her voice disappeared.

When Raven finally made it to the canteen and looked around, he saw her sitting at a table at the far end with a bunch of other girls. He took his tray of fish fingers and baked beans, went to get a drink of water, and was bumped into by someone behind him, almost sending his meal flying.

'Oi, look out, Brett, you dick!' Kyle laughed. 'Hi, Raven, how're you doing? Come and sit with us – we'll look after you. Brett, get me some water, will you?'

Raven backed away. 'It's OK, I'm going to sit over there . . .'

Kyle wore a frown, but almost instantly erased it with a smile. 'What's up? Hey, are you scared of us? Brett, look at that, you're scaring him off with all your crazy talk! Here' – he grabbed Raven's tray – 'sit with us, this is the cool dudes' table!'

Raven sat, heart thudding, at the empty table. Kyle and Brett took up seats opposite. There was a silence. Raven shoved a forkful of baked beans into his mouth so that he wouldn't have to make conversation. Kyle glanced at Brett.

'So, d'you have a sister called Parrot?' Brett asked.

'Brett!' Kyle exclaimed indulgently. 'Why would he have a sister called Parrot? That would sound stupid!'

'Stupider than Raven?' Brett said under his breath.

Kyle snorted with laughter but quickly turned it into a cough. 'Hey, wanna be part of our gang?'

'Oi!' Brett protested.

'No, it's OK, Raven's cool, aren't you, Raven?' He leaned forward. 'It's a secret gang. We meet every lunch break behind the changing rooms at the bottom of the playground. If you wanna be in it, meet us there at one fifteen. OK?'

Raven nodded numbly.

'Cool. Now get lost.'

Raven looked at him in surprise.

'Get lost!' Kyle hissed. 'If you're going to be in our gang, we can't be seen sitting together or people will start to get suspicious.'

Brett snorted again. Raven picked up his tray and carried it to a half-empty table at the other side of the cafeteria. When he glanced up again, he saw that Kyle and Brett were looking at each other and laughing.

He didn't go to the back of the changing rooms at break. Kyle and Brett might think he was gullible, but he wasn't an utter fool. Instead he went to the gap in the fence to say hello to Ella as he had promised. She might be an annoying attention-seeking brat, but she was the only one so far who genuinely seemed to give a damn about him. To his dismay, he found she had brought four of her friends along for the occasion.

'That's my new big brother,' Ella said excitedly. 'He's called Raven. He sleeps in the bedroom next door to mine. D'you like your new school, Raven? D'you have a nice teacher?'

He nodded and forced a smile.

'I'm going to play with my new skipping rope now,' Ella informed him. 'See you at home time!'

He waved to her and wandered back to the top of the playground, and waited for the rest of the hour to crawl by.

'How was school?' was the first thing Jackie asked as she met him at the gate, Ella in tow.

'OK.'

'Did you make any nice friends?'

Raven thought of Lotte, Kyle and Brett and shrugged.

'What are your teachers like?'

'OK.'

'Was the work easy? Hard?'

'OK.'

'Raven came to see me at the gap in the fence at lunch break,' Ella piped up as they got into the car.

Jackie shot Raven a surprised look. 'Really? That was nice of him!'

'Yes, I showed him to Lucy, Danielle and Shannon.'

'Oh, and did they approve?'

'Yes, but Danielle said did he come out of your tummy?'

'Oh!'

'And so I said, no, he's my *foster* brother, silly.'

'Oh . . .'

*   *   *

Back at the house, Jackie put out some snacks, Ella started colouring and Raven went upstairs with the excuse of homework. He entered his bedroom: he felt as if he had left it a lifetime ago and noticed that his bed had been remade and the curtains tied back. He let his bag fall to the ground and slid down the door until he was sitting on the carpet with his head on his knees. A thick web of exhaustion descended over him, so strong that just kicking off his shoes and taking off his blazer and tie seemed a monumental effort. For a while he just pressed his closed eyelids against his kneecaps, watching the fuzzy patterns of colours retreat into themselves like a kaleidoscope, thankful to be able to shut out the sharp outside world at last, grateful for this near oblivion. Gradually, though, his brain began to chug into life again, small pieces of his day flashing through his mind like a film trailer: Jackie knocking on the headmaster's door, the battered book landing on his desk, Lotte's purple nails, Brett frowning and saying 'Raving?' Kyle's laughing face at lunch, Ella and her groupies at the fence . . .

'Raven, dinner time!' Ella's authoritative voice rang out from downstairs. Raven sat up, startled. He didn't feel as if he had slept, or as if any time had passed at all, but when he looked at the clock, he realized that he had been sitting there for well over an hour. Disorientated, he got to his feet, blinded himself with the light switch and closed the curtains. Ella called again and he felt a wave of frustration rise. He couldn't face downstairs – the hot, steamy kitchen, the smell of food, Ella's chatter and Dan's questions. Dinner would drag on and then he still had to read a whole chapter of *To Kill a Mockingbird*, do a page of maths and finish colouring in the sea on some stupid map. That would take him up to – what – nine o'clock and then he would go to bed and fall asleep and wake up to the sound of his alarm and the whole nightmare of a day would start all over again.

He went downstairs into the warm fug of the kitchen, where Ella was running about with pieces of paper and Jackie was juggling hot plates. 'Would you give Ella a hand laying the table?'

Raven stopped, realizing that he didn't even know where the cutlery was kept and Jackie was too busy to be asked and Ella was under the table. He felt something akin to despair rise in his throat and tried a few drawers for luck before he felt a hand on his shoulder and heard, 'Here you go – top drawer by the fridge.' Raven gratefully took the handful of knives and forks from Dan's hand. But Dan didn't release his shoulder straight away.

'You OK?'

'Yeah.' Raven nodded quickly and pulled away.

At dinner Dan talked about plans for the weekend, Ella talked about how she had been made star of the day yet *again*, and Jackie talked about how Ella was going to suffer from malnutrition and stunted growth if she didn't finish her broccoli. Raven ate robotically, head propped up on his hand. When he finally escaped the kitchen, he lay on his bed and gazed dully at Chapter Five of *To Kill a Mockingbird* and wondered if there was any point at all in starting a book partway through or whether he could possibly bear to skim-read the first four chapters before even getting started on his actual homework. He decided that both options were equally ridiculous and so dropped the book back into his bag and got stuck into his maths instead. Then there was a knock on the door, and after a pause Dan put his head round.

'Can I come in?'

'Yes.'

He came and sat on the end of the bed, leaned back against the wall and stretched out his legs.

'Whoa, what a knackering day at the office. I had some very rude people shouting at me down the phone. I was so fed up by lunch time, all I could think about was coming home and seeing you lot.'

Raven eyed him warily.

'How was your day?' There it came.

'OK.'

Dan raised his eyebrows. 'Wanna tell me about it?'

Raven shook his head.

'Is that blood on your shirt sleeve?'

Raven glanced down at his arm. 'Yeah . . .'

'What happened?'

'Nose bleed.' He lied easily.

'Want some help with your homework?'

'No thanks.'

'Will you come downstairs and find me if you change your mind?'

'OK.'

Chapter Three

'Hi,' said Lotte, coming over to his desk as he packed up his bag after the last lesson of the morning.

Raven shot her a brief glance. 'Hi.'

Lotte stayed put, one hand on his desk, chewing the inside of her lip. 'Listen,' she said quickly, 'I think I should warn you. I overheard Kyle and Brett when you were out of class this morning and they—'

'Hey!' There was a shout from the doorway and he looked up with a start. The classroom had emptied and Kyle was flicking the light switch on and off. 'Lotte's got a boyfriend, a boyfriend, a boyfriend . . .'

Lotte rolled her eyes and stepped away from Raven with an irritated sigh. 'Grow up, Kyle.'

Kyle strode quickly over. 'Whaddya hassling him about then? Hey? Hey?'

He blocked her way as she tried to sidestep him out of the room.

'Nothing, Kyle, just leave me alone.'

Kyle's teasing grin suddenly disappeared. 'Whaddya bin tellin' him? Hey? Hey?'

But Lotte just swore, pushed past him and marched off.

Kyle seemed to hesitate, as if unsure whether to go after her. Then he looked at Raven and switched the grin back on. 'Let's go and have lunch,' he said.

In the canteen Raven got his food ahead of Kyle and Brett and walked quickly to a busy table and sat down. Predictably, Brett came after him and leaned over him, hands on the edge of the table.

'Hey, *Raving*, I think Kyle said you was to sit with us.'

Raven took a mouthful of processed peas. 'I'll sit where I want to sit,' he said.

There was a sudden silence at the table. All eyes seemed to have turned to him.

Brett hesitated, then put on a smile. 'You've just made a very big mistake,' he said. Leaning forward, he spat in Raven's plate and moved swiftly away.

Needless to say, Raven didn't eat any lunch. At break he leaned against the fence in a position from which he could keep an eye on the clock.

'Someone's looking for you.' Kyle made him start.

'Over by the gap in the fence,' Kyle went on. 'That little girl says you're her brother.'

Raven glanced down towards the end of the fence and saw Ella waving at him frantically.

He hesitated.

'C'mon!' Kyle said. 'She sent me over to get you. She's a cutie. I wish I had a little sister like her!'

Raven began to move down the playground towards the gap in the fence, Kyle following close behind. 'Hey, cutie!' Kyle said. 'Look who I've brought you!'

Ella sucked in her lower lip and looked shyly at the ground. She had two new friends with her today, both watching Raven with interest.

'Hi, Ella,' Raven mumbled quickly, patted her awkwardly on the head and started to move away.

Ella grabbed him by the shirt-tails. 'Who's he?' she said in a loud stage whisper, looking at Kyle.

'Hi, little Ella! I'm Kyle,' said Kyle, squatting down.

Ella smiled bashfully at him.

'Is Raven your big brother then?'

She nodded. 'He's my foster brother,' she said proudly.

Kyle laughed. 'Your *fuster* brother? What's a *fuster* brother?'

Raven felt a sinking feeling in the pit of his stomach. 'Ella, why don't you—?'

'It means he didn't come out from my mummy's tummy.'

'Really?' Kyle choked back a laugh.

'I'm going now, Ella,' Raven said in a rush. 'Come on, Kyle.'

'Hold on, hold on, I wanna talk to your little sister. So whose tummy did he come out of then?'

Ella put her finger in her mouth. 'I don't know . . . I think – I think another mummy's.'

'And what happened to her?'

'Ella!' Raven shouted.

'She died,' Ella said.

'Hey! Hey!' Kyle ran down the corridor shouting after Raven, but Raven took the stairs two at a time, determined to lose him. He reached the floor above and sprinted down two more corridors, the blood thudding in his face, his breath rasping. He heard a teacher shouting at Kyle on the stairs and, thinking he had lost him, ducked into a classroom. But moments later the door swung open.

'Raven! Jesus, man—'

'Just leave me alone!'

'Listen, I'm sorry, all right? I didn't know about that stuff . . .'

Raven turned to face the wall, struggling to pull himself together.

Kyle came closer. Raven moved away.

'Listen, that really sucks. I'm sorry, mate.' Kyle sounded almost genuine.

Raven pressed the balls of his hands against his eyelids to hold back the tears.

'You know, Brett's a dickhead,' Kyle declared suddenly. 'I saw what he did to you at lunch. He's just jealous 'cos he knows I wanna be best mates with you and not with him any more. It's pathetic.'

Raven brought his hands down from his face. 'I don't believe you!' he snapped angrily.

'I'm not lying, man! When you first arrived yesterday, I said to Brett, "That guy seems nice – maybe we should let him in our club," and Brett went all weird and started saying nasty stuff about you. When I saw what Brett did to you at lunch, I told him I didn't want him in my gang no more an' he got all upset, but I said, "No way, man, Raven's my friend an' you don't go picking on my friends." So Brett an' I ain't friends no more. So I want you to be my new best mate. You wanna be my new best mate?'

Raven looked at him, eyes wide, the air still rasping in his throat. The sudden change in Kyle was distinctly suspicious. He didn't know what to think and all of a sudden felt incredibly tired.

'Come on,' Kyle said. 'We can be mates, can't we? We can sit together in class an' have lunch together an' stuff. You can come over to my place after school an' we can kick back with a DVD or play on my computer . . .'

Raven looked at him warily.

'Honest,' Kyle said. 'I don't want to have nuffin' to do with that shithead Brett.'

'OK,' Raven said dubiously.

Kyle's smile broadened. 'Cool!' he exclaimed. 'We'll be best mates an' I'll look out for you an' I'll never let Brett piss you off again.'

Raven forced a conciliatory smile. Perhaps Kyle was all right after all. 'OK,' he said again.

For the rest of the day Kyle didn't leave his side. They ignored Brett, who sat on his own looking sullen, and during the interminable RE class Kyle passed Raven rude limericks and dirty jokes. One about a nun and a Dutchman was so funny, Raven actually laughed out loud.

The afternoon went by quickly, and at the last bell Kyle gave Raven a piece of paper with a scribbled number on it. 'You can ring me any time 'cos I got a phone in my room,' he told Raven. 'I also got my own DVD player, an' my brother works at Blockbuster's so I can get any film I want for free. If you want, you can come over at the weekend and we can get a takeaway an' stay up all night watchin' DVDs. That's what I used to do with Brett, but I'm gonna do it with you now. Then on Saturday we'll go into town and I'll show you all the cool places to hang out.'

'You've got a good appetite all of a sudden,' Dan remarked at dinner.

'I'm hungry,' Raven said.

'I can see that. Aren't they feeding you properly at school?'

Raven thought back to lunch and then banished it from his mind. From now on he'd be sitting with Kyle, and Brett would never dare bother him again.

'Raven's got a nice friend,' Jackie said.

'He's called Kyle,' Ella added.

Dan's eyes widened in surprise. 'Kyle, eh? Is he in your class?'

Raven nodded. 'First I thought he was kind of an idiot,' he said. 'But actually he's all right, and *really* funny.'

Dan looked amazed. He exchanged looks with his wife. 'That's great, Raven,' he said. 'That's great, really great! So what did you and Kyle get up to today?'

'He wants me to spend the night at his house at the weekend.'

Dan and Jackie exchanged looks again. 'Well – I'm sure that can be arranged. If you ask him for his number, we can give his parents a ring and—'

'I've got his number,' Raven said.

'Oh! OK, well, do you want us to give them a call tonight or do you want to have some time to think about it?'

'You can call them tonight,' Raven said. 'If you want,' he added quickly.

'OK, we'll do that.' Dan smiled. 'And maybe the following weekend he can come over here.'

'What about me?' Ella whined. 'I don't want Raven to go away already!'

'It's just for one night, munchkin! How about we invite Lucy over while he's away?'

Raven decided to tackle *To Kill a Mockingbird* that evening. He didn't have much other homework and although he was tired, he didn't feel like going to bed. He started speed-reading from Chapter One but by the fourth page had slowed down to normal pace as he began to be drawn in by the characters and the plot. Somewhere in Chapter Three he decided that it would be much nicer to read in bed and so stripped down to his boxers, brushed his teeth and turned off the main light, switching on his bedside one and pulling the duvet over his head. Somewhere in Chapter Four he fell asleep.

'Did you call them?' he asked Dan at breakfast the next morning.

'Yeah, buddy, I did, but I think your pal Kyle must have made a mistake. The number he wrote down was a pizza delivery place.'

Raven looked at him. 'Are you sure?'

'Yes, I dialled it three times! Never mind, you can ask him for it again today. It's surprising the amount of people who don't know their own phone number!'

'I know my own phone number,' Ella said.

'You made a mistake with your phone number,' he told Kyle in the playground before the first bell.

Kyle looked at him, then widened his eyes in surprise. 'You phoned me last night?'

'My foster dad did. He wanted to check with your parents if it was OK for this weekend.'

'Oh, shit, I probably gave you my old number by mistake. We only moved last month.'

'No, it was a pizza place.'

'Really?'

'Yes.'

'Oh, sorry, mate. I'll give you the right one when we get to class. So, can you come this weekend?'

'They said yes.'

'Cool! OK, I'm gonna plan all kinds of fun stuff. You gotta tell me what DVDs you wanna watch, OK? And tell me all your favourite food. I'll get my mum to buy it.'

They sat together all day again and Kyle drew a very funny and rather rude sketch of Mr Rumbold on the back of Raven's pencil case. At lunch break Raven showed Kyle a note he had found in his blazer pocket that read: *Raven, will you go out with me? from Sophie xxx*, and Kyle ran off to torment Sophie about it. In PE they partnered each other, freezing in white shorts and T-shirts, bouncing muddy basketballs across the puddles in the playground.

'What happened to your arms?' Kyle asked him.

'Got scratched by a cat,' Raven replied.

'Shit. Must've been *some cat*,' Kyle said.

As they were changing back into their uniforms, Kyle asked Raven, 'So, why did your mother die?'

Buttoning his shirt, Raven hesitated for a moment. He looked at Kyle carefully. But Kyle looked genuinely interested.

'You have to promise not to tell anyone,' Raven warned him.

'OK.'

'She was murdered,' Raven said. 'And I know who did it.'

Kyle's eyes widened. 'Really? What are you going to do about it?'

'I'm figuring out a plan,' Raven replied.

Jackie was waiting as usual with Ella at the gate. 'Hi, lovey, did you have a good day?'

'Yep.'

'Great! What did you do?'

'We had PE this afternoon. We played dodgeball. And Kyle's given me the right number this time.'

As Raven was getting into the car, Jackie suddenly said, 'Raven, your tie.'

He felt for where it should have been. 'Oh . . .'

'Do you know where you might have left it?'

'In the changing rooms . . .'

'Perhaps you'd better run back and get it.'

'OK.' He dumped his bag and made his way with difficulty back up the street and against the mass exodus at the gate. Then he ran across the emptying playground to the changing rooms, found his tie beneath the bench, grabbed it and ran out again. As he neared the gate, he suddenly stopped. Two boys were walking out ahead of him, bags slung over their shoulders, shirts hanging out of their trousers, jostling each other and laughing. They crossed the road, still talking, then disappeared from sight. Kyle and Brett. Unmistakably.

Chapter Four

There was probably a logical explanation. Or so Raven told himself that evening as he tried to concentrate on his homework. Maybe after the last bell Brett had gone over to Kyle to apologize. Maybe Kyle had decided they could all three be friends. Maybe Brett had decided that Raven was all right after all. But the churned-up feeling in the pit of his stomach wouldn't leave.

At dinner time he gave Dan the new number Kyle had scribbled down for him. He hoped that at least Brett wouldn't be invited at the weekend too. Kyle had suggested Raven call him. Maybe after Dan had spoken to the parents and it was all confirmed, he could call Kyle and find out if Brett was going to be there. Or maybe Dan would be able to find out for him.

When the knock on his door came, he started. Dan

came in looking thoughtful. He sat down on the end of Raven's bed, the piece of paper with the phone number between his fingers.

'I have a nasty little feeling your friend Kyle's pulling your leg,' he said.

Raven looked at him hotly. 'What?'

'This number, Raven, is for a *Chinese takeaway*.' Dan looked annoyed.

Raven felt his heartbeat pick up. 'Maybe – maybe he lives there! Maybe his parents work there or something.'

Dan shook his head. 'No, I checked, and only a Chinese family lives there. Kyle isn't Chinese, is he?'

Raven felt the blood pound in his face. 'No.'

Dan's face was serious. 'Look, buddy, I think Kyle's a bit of a joker. And I think someone needs to have a word with him. So I'm going to take you to school tomorrow and you can point him out to me and—'

'No!' Raven's voice began to rise. 'He just made a mistake! He said – he said he wasn't sure of his number! He – he said he'd only just moved house and – and . . .' It was difficult to talk.

Dan touched his arm. 'OK, easy. If you don't want me to interfere, that's fine. Kyle's just probably having a bit of fun. But if he hasn't come clean with you by tomorrow—'

'He will! He said he was sorry already!'

'All right,' said Dan, infuriatingly calm. 'Just make sure you let him know that one practical joke is more than enough.'

Raven slept badly. When he got to school the next morning, neither Kyle nor Brett were in the playground. When he got to class, they were both sitting together at the back.

'Sorry,' said Brett as Raven walked up to them. 'This seat's saved.'

Raven ignored him. 'Hi,' he said to Kyle.

Kyle looked up with a smirk. 'Do I know you?'

Raven stared at him. 'What are you doing?'

Kyle leaned back in his chair. 'What am I doing?' he drawled. 'I'm sitting with my best mate and telling you to piss off, that's what.'

Brett snorted with laughter. Raven turned round and moved away, only to find that there were no other empty seats. He stopped still, breathing hard.

Mr Rumbold came in. 'Right, books out, page ninety-five. Raven, *sit down*, will you? Lotte, read the first question.'

Cheeks burning, Raven moved back towards the last empty desk beside Kyle.

Kyle put his leg across the chair and looked up at Raven with a grin.

'Just move,' Raven whispered.

'You gotta be kidding,' Kyle said.

'What is going on at the back? Raven Winter, I told you to *sit down*!'

'I can't,' Raven said, his voice unsteady. 'He won't let me.'

'What are you doing?' Mr Rumbold shouted at Kyle.

'Oh, sir, we don't want to sit next to him, he smells!' Kyle said. Laughter.

Raven backed away, his cheeks burning.

'Sir, he never washes,' Brett added. 'He really stinks!' More laughter.

'I don't care!' Mr Rumbold shouted, marching over. He pointed to the chair. 'Sit!' he roared at Raven.

Raven sat. As Mr Rumbold made his way back to the top of the class, Brett held his nose and Kyle made gagging noises. There were more titters.

'Quiet!' Mr Rumbold roared.

Raven opened his textbook, blinking down at the page, and struggled to hold back the tears.

At first break Raven went numbly out into the play-ground. As the muffled screams rose around him, he was filled with a feeling of despair. The sun shone on the rain-soaked concrete and everything seemed too bright, too harsh, too real. Several boys splashed past him in pursuit of a ball. Raven pushed his hands into his pockets and leaned against the fence, looking at the clock. Five past eleven: another twenty-five minutes to go – he didn't know how he could bear it. All around him, voices rang out, shouting, calling, laughing, while he stood still in the eye of the storm, staring at the damn clock, waiting for it all to end. Suddenly he saw Kyle and Brett moving towards him. He looked away quickly. Better to pretend he hadn't seen them. But out of the corner of his eye he could tell they were heading straight for him, jostling each other and laughing. It was then that he realized he hadn't picked a particularly good spot to stand in. Without thinking he had wandered almost all the way down to the bottom of the playground, away from the school entrance where the teacher on duty and most of the sixth-formers hung out, with all the games of football going on in between.

'We haven't seen much of you lately, Raving. You scared of us or something?'

'Get lost.' He pushed past Kyle but Brett blocked his way along the fence and shoved him hard against the railings. Some other boys that Raven recognized from class stopped their football game and wandered over to see what was going on.

'Are you scared of us, Raving?' Kyle drawled, turning towards the other boys for a laugh. 'Hey, you guys!' he suddenly shouted across at the others. 'D'you wanna know why Raving's called Raving? He's a raving loony, that's why! He talks to himself and rolls his eyes and froths at the mouth!'

Snorts of laughter from behind. The football group came closer.

Raven tried to push past but Brett shoved him, hard. He stumbled backwards and almost fell. 'Did you really think Kyle wanted to be your friend?' he snorted. 'Did you really? Huh? Huh?' He laughed, then gave Raven a vicious kick on the shin. 'Answer me, you dick-head!'

Raven stumbled back. 'Why don't you just piss off!'

Brett raised his fist. 'If you don't talk, we can always make you!'

'Easy, Brett, easy.' Kyle laughed, slinging a heavy arm over Raven's shoulders. 'Raving's my little buddy – isn't that right, Raving? Isn't that right?' His hard green eyes bore sharply into him.

Raven gave Kyle a shove. Kyle nodded at Brett and

suddenly Brett grabbed Raven by the arm and twisted his hand right up behind him, pinning him back against the railings.

'Isn't that right?' Kyle said again.

'Get your fucking hands off me!' Raven writhed in Brett's iron grip.

'He's been trying to call me on the phone for two days,' Kyle said to the other boys. 'Isn't that right, Raving?'

Titters.

'And what happened then? What happened when your dad – your *pretend dad* – tried to call?'

Raven held his breath in pain. Brett twisted his arm harder. 'Answer him, you idiot!'

Raven screwed up his eyes and tried to kick Brett's legs. But Brett only twisted his arm further, forcing him to freeze. 'Answer the question or I'll break your fucking arm!'

'It was the wrong number!'

'What number, idiot?'

'A pizza place.' Laughter.

'And then?'

'I don't give a damn—!'

'And then?'

'And – and then a restaurant . . .' It was hard to think.

His arm was in agony. There was more laughter. Brett's was the loudest.

'And why did your pretend dad call?'

Raven hesitated. Brett gave his arm another wrench and pain shot through his shoulder like lightning. 'He – he wanted to speak to your parents,' Raven managed from between clenched teeth.

'*Why?*'

'You know why!' Raven suddenly shouted. 'Stop trying to make a fool of me just so you can show off in front of your friends!'

Kyle's eyes darkened and Brett wrenched Raven's arm so hard that he fell to his knees.

'Why did he call?' Kyle demanded again. 'Was it because you wanted to come to my house this weekend? Was it? Was it?'

Brett and some of the other boys fell about laughing.

Raven felt tears of pain spring to his eyes.

'Why are you crying, Raving?' said Kyle. 'Is it because you miss your mumsy-wumsy?'

'Fuck off!'

'Oh, poor baby!' Kyle crowed. 'Look, everyone. Raven's crying!'

Suddenly the bell went, startling them all. Brett let go of his wrist and his arm went numb.

Kyle swung an arm over Raven's shoulder. 'So you still wanna be my friend?' He laughed.

As soon as they got to class, Raven grabbed a seat at the back, as far away as possible from Kyle and Brett, and lowered his head behind the kid in front, trying to sort himself out. Pain shot down his arm in nauseating waves, and when he tried to pick up his pen, it fell out from between his fingers. A tear escaped down his cheek and he swiped at it, willing himself to get a grip. Mr Miles, the whiskery, bespectacled history teacher, banged his case down on the desk, shouted at them all to be quiet and then told them to open their books at Chapter Eight.

'New boy, start reading,' he barked.

Raven closed his eyes and pressed the heel of his hands hard against his lids. There was a long silence.

'New boy, paragraph one, Chapter Eight!'

'I think his name is Raving, sir.' Brett's voice. Nervous laughter.

'Be quiet, Brett! Are you asleep at the back?'

More laughter. Raven took his hands away from his eyes. Gazed down at the watery blurred print of the page in front of him. Took a deep breath and began to read. He only managed to get to the end of the third line before Mr Miles stopped him. 'Stop, stop. For goodness' sake, what's the matter with you?'

Silence. Raven pressed his palms back against his eyes.

'I think he's crying, sir,' somebody said.

'What on earth is going on? Do you need to go and see the nurse?'

Raven shook his head.

'Sir, I think I know what the matter is.' Kyle's voice was low, subdued. 'His mum was *murdered*.'

Kyle and Brett raced out of the class at the lunch bell while Raven took his time putting his books away, keeping his head carefully lowered. He was aware of someone approaching him but didn't look up for fear that it was Kyle or Brett returning to taunt him.

'Hi,' said a voice. It was Lotte.

Raven risked a glance. Her friend Alice was waiting nervously in the doorway.

'Are you OK?'

He shrugged.

'Kyle and Brett are just the scum of the earth. You should complain to the head,' Lotte said.

Raven just shrugged again, zipping up his bag.

'You really should. They always pick on anyone who's new. But they eventually get bored of it. In the meantime, if you want to sit with us at lunch or whatever, you're welcome.'

And get taunted for having a girlfriend? Raven thought bitterly, but he managed a wry smile. 'Thanks.'

'No problem. See you later.' She joined Alice and they left.

At dinner that evening he told Dan that Kyle's family were going away for the weekend, and so the sleepover was off. Dan looked unconvinced but didn't pursue it. Jackie dished up, Dan untied his tie and rolled up his shirt sleeves and Ella chattered on and on. 'And Miss Mann said, "Ella, you will be the White Rabbit." And I said, "I don't *want* to be the White Rabbit, the White Rabbit just goes, *I'm late, I'm late*. I want to be Alice in Wonderland." But Miss Mann said, "Ella, you're being difficult." And I said, "I'm not being difficult! I just think Freddie should be the White Rabbit 'cos he's got sticking-out teeth!" And Miss Mann said, "Ella, that's enough." So I don't like Miss Mann any more, Mummy. I want to move to another class!'

Raven suddenly wished he was five again, when all you had to worry about were things like what part you had in the school play. Jackie and Dan laughed indulgently at Ella, and he suddenly wanted to scream. Their love for her was so obvious, so transparent. They were already such a family. What part would he ever have to play in this happy-clappy scene?

'But the White Rabbit's a very important part.' Jackie was trying to reason with Ella. 'The White Rabbit is the one who leads Alice to Wonderland in the first place. Without the White Rabbit there wouldn't be any story.'

'I think you'd make an excellent White Rabbit,' Dan added.

'But I don't look like a rabbit, I look like Alice,' Ella countered. 'I've got yellow hair just like Alice. Mummy, don't you think I look like Alice? If I have my hair back in a hairband like this? Look, Mummy, look!'

Raven ate his meal in silence. Every mouthful threatened to stick in his throat.

The next day he got up, showered and dressed like a robot. In class, he sat as far away as possible from Kyle and Brett. At lunch he sat at an almost empty table and ate with his head down. During break he walked up and down the top of the playground, dodging the heavy, wet balls. Back in class, he read, he listened, he wrote as the ghastly day ground on and on. And it hurt just to breathe.

That night Ella burst into his bedroom, brandishing

a piece of paper. 'I drew a picture for you—' She froze, staring at his arm, the smile dying on her lips. Her blue eyes widened. 'What are you doing?' she gasped.

'Nothing,' Raven replied quickly.

She drew in a deep breath. 'I made a picture for you in class today,' she said quietly, turning the crumpled piece of paper towards him.

'Oh. Thanks.'

'It's a picture of me,' Ella went on, her eyes still wide. 'It's me in the school play as Alice in Wonderland. Miss Mann was cross when I showed it to her. She said I was *trying*.' She laid the drawing carefully on his bed. 'What does *trying* mean?'

'Annoying,' Raven said. 'Tiring, irritating, a pain in the neck. I thought you were going to be the White Rabbit.'

'Well, we'll see about that.' Ella began to stare again. 'Raven?'

'What?'

'Shall I get you a plaster?'

'No.'

'OK. I'll draw you another picture then. I'll draw you a picture of Freddie as the White Rabbit. OK?' She smiled at him hopefully.

'OK,' he said.

She went out quietly, pulling the door closed behind her. Raven returned his gaze to his penknife and drew another long scratch, watching it turn from white to red across the inside of his arm.

Chapter Five

'Homework. Well, poems are meant to be shared, so who wants to start?' Mrs Harrison placed her bag on the desk and began cleaning the board. There was a collective groan from the class. 'Benny?'

Trying to look embarrassed but failing, the teacher's pet came to the front and opened his exercise book. *'To my grandmother,'* he began, with a self-conscious grin. *'Her brown eyes hold secrets of years gone by and stories never told . . .'*

Raven looked at his watch and realized that he had another seven hours to get through, another seven hours of school, before being able to walk out of the gates. History, then maths, then French, then science, then lunch, then PE . . . It seemed impossible, impossible it would ever come to an end.

'Raven Winter, your turn.' He was jolted back to the classroom by the sound of his name. He looked at Mrs Harrison's smiling face, and a cold, sinking feeling descended over him. He picked up his exercise book and got up slowly, as if moving through porridge. Kyle and Brett had already started tittering before he reached the front. He turned to face the class, opened his book and stared down hotly at the four scrawled lines.

> *'I sit at my desk, I do as I must,*
> *my heart is ridden with pain.*
> *I follow instructions without looking up,*
> *quietly going insane.'*

There was a stunned silence as he went to sit down. Even Kyle and Brett were quiet. Then Mrs Harrison cleared her throat and said, 'Right, thank you, Raven. Who's next?'

As Raven reached the playground after the last bell, the heavens opened and he was forced to run all the way to the bus shelter, his blazer over his head. On Thursdays and Fridays, when he finished an hour later than Ella, Dan and Jackie let him take the bus home. Just his luck that on that day it would choose to pour.

Beneath the dripping bus shelter, he perched on the plastic bench, watching the rain drum steadily around him. Over the road, pupils streaked across the playground, coats or bags held over their heads. Traffic crawled by, bumper to bumper in a sea of red lights. A figure in a pink hood suddenly came charging towards the shelter to get out of the rain, collapsing onto the bench beside him. The figure pulled off its hood, revealing a mane of tangled blonde hair.

Damp-cheeked and pink-nosed, Lotte gazed at him in surprise. 'I never knew you took the bus.'

'Only Thursdays and Fridays,' Raven replied, and turned to peer up the road for it.

'Oh,' Lotte said. She dropped her school bag at her feet and ineffectually pushed back the wet hair from her face.

There was a long silence. Raven stared through the driving rain at the traffic, willing the bus to come into view.

'I liked your poem,' Lotte said suddenly.

He waited for the snigger, but it didn't come. 'I mean – that's exactly how it is. You said it in two sentences. It was perfect. I've written it down. Whenever my parents ask me how my day was, that's what I'm going to say in reply.'

Raven felt the colour rise to his cheeks and he looked down at the ground.

'I hate school too,' Lotte said. 'The petty rules, the endless repetition, the utter senselessness of it all.'

Raven glanced at her uncertainly. 'You don't seem to.'

Lotte gave a small laugh. 'Are you kidding me? Just because I hang around with Alice and Debbie and that stupid lot? All they ever talk about are boring soaps and blokes they fancy—' She went pink suddenly and glanced away. 'Anyway, it's always the same thing, and it's so bloody depressing.'

There was another long silence. Raven scuffed the toe of his shoe against the concrete and looked down at the ground.

'Don't you sometimes just wish you could go to sleep and fast-forward the next few years of school, of exams, of finding a job, and just wake up and find you're an adult?' Lotte asked him.

Raven looked at her. 'Yes,' he said.

She seemed surprised. 'Really?'

'There's so much to do in the next five years,' Raven said quietly. 'And all for what? Once we finally get there, once we have the job and the house and the family, we just sit there and wait for it all to be taken away from us again.'

Lotte frowned. 'What d'you mean?'

'We wait to die,' Raven said.

'What?'

'The job, the house, the family, all that. It's just a distraction. A distraction to keep us from facing the fact that it's all going to end.'

'Don't you believe in God?'

Raven looked at her in surprise. 'No. Do you?'

She heaved a sigh. 'I suppose not. I used to though. My parents used to take me and my brother to church now and again, and we even went to Sunday school for a while. But deep down I don't think my parents really believed in all that stuff themselves. They just try to hold onto it because the alternative, I guess, is too unbearable.'

'And so why don't you?'

Lotte gave a small shrug. 'I just woke up one day and realized it was a load of rubbish. Kind of like suddenly realizing Father Christmas doesn't really exist. Father Christmas is a character adults invented in order to make kids happy. God is a character adults invented to make themselves happy.'

'Exactly,' Raven said.

'What about you?' Lotte asked him. 'Did you ever believe in God?'

'Yes. Not in God as a man dressed in white sitting on a cloud, but in the concept of there being some kind of Creator – yes.'

'When did you stop believing?' Lotte asked.

'When my mother died,' Raven said.

The weather got colder and every day seemed to start with rain. Sometimes it rained all day. The worst days were when he woke up to the sound of rain, when morning was nothing more than a watery grey sky, when darkness fell mid afternoon and when PE meant freezing in white shorts and T-shirt in a muddy playground with Kyle and Brett doing everything they could to hit him with the basketball. Days when they had 'wet break' weren't much better: three hundred pupils cooped up in the lunch hall, their voices boxed in and magnified against the walls, muddy footprints everywhere, the girls sitting round the edges with their highlighter pens and sparkly padlocked notebooks, the boys tearing about in the middle, jostling and throwing and skidding and tripping, trampling blazers underfoot and getting shouted at by the harassed-looking teacher on duty. On swimming days there were cold wet changing rooms and slippery floors, toes curled around the side of the pool, goggles and flat blue water, then the whistle, a dive and icy shock. Breast stroke, crawl or backstroke to the other side, turn and back, turn and back, turn and back. Out again and queuing for the showers, damp towel and shivering, sodden underwear trampled underfoot, spiky hair and pink, watery eyes. In the car on the way home, Ella whining, rivulets racing down the windows, a sea of red brake lights and Jackie moaning . . . Except for Thursdays and Fridays.

'What a shit day,' Lotte greeted him as usual.

Raven shrugged and sat down on the plastic bench. 'Yeah.'

Lotte looked at him expectantly.

He looked back.

'Sometimes I just wish something would happen,' she went on. 'Something exciting, you know? Something out of the ordinary. I'm so sick of the same old routine, day after day. My life is so boring.'

Raven said nothing.

Lotte cocked her head. 'You don't talk much, do you?'

He felt the colour rise to his cheeks.

'It's just that most people – well – chat,' she explained. 'And you don't.'

'So?'

She shrugged. 'So nothing. Some people in class say

stuff about you . . .' She trailed off, appearing embarrassed suddenly.

He looked at her, hard. 'What kind of stuff?'

'You know . . .' She looked awkward for a moment.
'Just stupid gossip and stuff.'

'About what?'

'About how fucked up you are. Because of what
happened to your mum. And because you never talk to
anyone, even though all the girls fancy you.'

'Huh?'

'I mean' – Lotte's cheeks flared momentarily – 'not *all*
the girls, but, you know, the others . . .' She stared
intently at the ground.

There was a sudden silence.

'Some people think I'm weird too,' Lotte went on, as
if to make amends. 'Just because I don't like their kind of
music and prefer books to silly teen magazines.'

They boarded the bus in silence. Raven followed Lotte
up to the top deck and, after a moment's hesitation, took
the empty seat behind her.

'What books do you like then?' he asked.

She turned in her seat to look round at him. 'Books
about real life. I don't mean biographies. Just books
about things that really happen. Books which don't have
happy endings.'

'You should read *The Outsiders* then,' Raven said.

Lotte's eyes widened. 'I *love* that book.'

Raven looked at her in surprise. 'Have you read the others?' he asked. '*Rumble Fish, That Was Then, This Is Now*—'

'I've read them all,' Lotte told him. '*Rumble Fish* was my favourite.'

'Mine too,' Raven agreed. 'The ending was brilliant.'

'You should read *Looking for JJ*,' Lotte said. 'I've just finished it. It's about a girl who kills her best friend when she's just a child, and then has to go into hiding when she gets out of prison because everyone is out to get her. The ending is so moving. So real.'

Raven stared at her.

'It sounds gruesome but it's really not,' Lotte went on. 'You really feel for this girl. The murder wasn't really her fault. You'll see what I mean when you read it. I'll lend it to you if you like.'

Raven swallowed and nodded. 'OK,' he said.

The next morning, before the first bell, Lotte came up to him, pulling something out from beneath her coat. 'Here.'

He looked down. It was a book. *The* book. He took it. It looked brand new.

'I bought it for you because my copy's all creased and dog-eared and crappy,' Lotte said quickly. 'Anyway, I hope you enjoy it.' Before he had time to thank her, she had rejoined her friend. It wasn't until lunch that he opened the cover to start reading and saw the inscription. *To Raven, love from Lotte xxx.* For some strange reason it made a lump rise in his throat.

Kyle and Brett were on his case. They had seen Lotte give him the book that morning, and so spent all day tormenting him. In maths Brett stuck his foot out while Raven was walking up to the front of the class to answer a question on the board. In English Kyle knocked Raven's ruler onto the floor as he was walking back to his desk and then quickly stepped on it and broke it. In science Kyle helped himself to Raven's pen and then refused to return it, saying he had never borrowed it, so Raven had to write out all the experiments in green biro and then got shouted at by Mr Davis when he collected up the books. When the home bell went, they jostled him in the corridor, making the most of the emptying school.

'You looking for your *girlfriend*, Raving? You and your girlfriend going on a date this evening?'

Raven ignored him and headed quickly down the

stairs, but Kyle and Brett were behind him in an instant, shoving him, trying to trip him up, continuing with the girlfriend taunts. As they reached the playground, Raven hesitated. He didn't want to head straight for the bus stop and risk Kyle and Brett seeing him get on the bus with Lotte. He needed to shake them off somehow. In the crowd of parents and pupils at the gate, he managed to lose sight of them for a moment. Quickly doubling back, he headed for the toilets at the side of the play-ground. From one of the cubicles at the back there was a small window which looked out onto the gate. From there he would be able to wait until he could see Kyle and Brett go home.

The toilets were smelly, empty and flooded with harsh yellow light. Raven went into the last cubicle, closed the painted blue door with a bang and drew the bolt. Then he jumped up onto the toilet lid and peered out of the tiny window. He froze. Kyle and Brett were no longer at the gate. They weren't walking down the street outside the school and they weren't in the playground. In fact Kyle and Brett were no longer to be seen at all. Either they had rushed off without bothering to try and find Raven again, which seemed unlikely. Or . . . Raven desperately scanned the heads milling round the gate, his eyes watering with the effort. He must have missed them – they had to be there still – he was just panicking, he needed to slow down and look! But his heart was beginning to thud painfully in his chest and a weird, shaky feeling crept over his whole body. The window was too small, and didn't open all the way. He was so stupid! He had gone and trapped himself!

He turned round on the toilet lid to face the cubicle door and check the bolt. It was drawn and it would say ENGAGED, so that was a dead giveaway. What should he do: buy himself time with a locked door which flagged up his exact location, or pull the bolt back and at least retain an element of surprise? One hand on each wall, he lowered himself to a squatting position, straining to hear beyond the hiss and gurgle of the leaky tap and the frantic thud of his panicked heart. And then he heard it. The squeak of trainers on the tiled floor. He knew he should try and run for it but his body seemed to have frozen. A sudden bang from the far end of the toilets made him jump. It was followed by another bang, then another. Somebody was kicking open the toilet doors one by one. As the bangs grew louder, Raven dug his teeth into his clenched fist. It was an effort just to breathe.

Suddenly there was silence.

'Oh, look.' Kyle's voice rang out from the other side of the bolted door. 'This one's locked.'

'I wonder who on earth could be inside.' Brett's voice was thick with suppressed laughter.

There was a violent banging. 'Open up, whoever you are!'

Another long silence. Raven held his breath.

Then suddenly there was an almighty crash. Raven gasped. Somebody had kicked the door so violently that a crack had appeared along the side.

'I don't think it would take us too long to break this door down, do you?' Kyle's voice.

Another crash, and another, and another. The blue paint around the bolt started to flake; several more cracks ran down the side of the door. Then silence again.

Raven clenched his teeth to stop them from chattering. His eyes were fixed on the large gap between the bottom of the door and the dirty yellow floor. It would take them seconds to slide underneath.

'Aaaaaarrhh!' Kyle and Brett's heads appeared simultaneously over the cubicle walls, one on each side. They burst into fits of laughter at each other and then at Raven as he stumbled forward off the toilet lid. And for a moment he thought it was going to be all right, that they were going to be content with having just scared him. But then they stopped laughing.

Raven jumped for the door and grabbed hold of the

bolt but it wouldn't budge. Kyle and Brett must have jammed it in some way. He shoved his school bag off his back and got down on all fours to slide under the door but Kyle saw what he was doing and, with a yell, swung himself over the cubicle wall and came down, feet first, on top of him. Then it was a confusion of arms, legs, kicks and shoves as Brett jumped in too. Within seconds Kyle had got Raven by the back of his shirt, half strangling him, while Brett knelt painfully on his back, pinning him to the wet floor.

'Hey, look here, it's our friend Raving! What are you doing here, Raving? What are you doing here all alone, hiding in the toilets? Were you waiting for your girlfriend, hey, Raving?'

Raven lashed out with his feet and elbows, trying to tear himself from Kyle's grasp and dragging himself to his feet. His foot met Brett's leg with a satisfying crack and Brett yelped. 'You little fuck!'

'Right, that's it,' Kyle said. 'I think he needs to cool down!' With a grunt, he twisted Raven's arm behind his back and forced him down to his knees. Brett managed to get hold of Raven's other arm and grabbed him by the hair. With a lot of puffing and swearing, they manoeuvred Raven towards the toilet seat and kicked up the lid.

'No!' Raven threw himself backwards with all his might but they only twisted his arms further up behind his back. He twisted his head one way and then the other, trying to bite his attackers, but a knee in his back forced him down to the floor and suddenly the white enamel of the toilet bowl was shooting towards him and water burst up in a deafening rush as Kyle pulled the chain. He resurfaced, choking, his face numb with shock, and then they were pushing him down again, banging his forehead against the cold enamel, pulling the chain again so that more water bubbled up, and he found himself trying to inhale even though he knew he shouldn't, and cold water shot in through his mouth and up his nose and he was coughing and retching, crumpled over the toilet bowl just trying to breathe. And then he heard a voice in the distance say, 'Shit, that sounded like Mrs Harrison,' followed by, 'Come on, let's get out of here,' and suddenly there was no hand on his head or knee in his back or hands gripping his arms and he fell back onto the floor, his head lolling against the cubicle door, and all he could do was cough and retch and spit and shudder.

When it finally seemed possible to move, he got back onto his knees and retched and spat again and again onto the floor. Then he grappled with the door, found it still jammed, and so kicked his bag out beneath it and then followed, sliding through the gap. At the basins he ran the hot tap, scalding himself with water, rubbing soap all over his face, his hair, his neck, even his tongue, rinsing his mouth out again and again until he didn't have the strength to do it any more. Then he took great wads of toilet paper from one of the cubicles and dried himself as best he could with hands that wouldn't stop shaking. His hair and blazer and shirt remained soaking, his nose wouldn't stop running and his teeth were chattering like gunfire inside his head. He threw all the wadded toilet paper in the bin, zipped up his coat, picked up his school bag and pulled up his sleeve to look at his watch, and when his eyes finally focused enough for him to make out the hands, he saw that it was already nearly five. He walked quickly out of the boys' toilets, scanned the empty playground in case Kyle and Brett were still hanging around, then hurried out of the school gate and towards the bus stop. The bright lights from the high street danced and bled and blurred together and a car hooted angrily at him. He felt as if he were walking strangely, jerkily, his legs not quite sure what they should be doing.

To his surprise, Lotte was still in the bus shelter,

arms folded against the cold, chin tucked into her blue scarf.

'What took you so long? Three buses have gone by already.'

'I didn't ask you to wait for me,' Raven snapped.

Lotte lifted her chin from her scarf and looked at him carefully.

Perching on the far end of the plastic bench, Raven thrust his hands into his pockets and looked down the road for the bus.

'I waited for you because you're the only halfway interesting person I get to talk to all day,' Lotte suddenly said.

Raven drew in his breath, ready for a sarcastic reply, and then burst into tears.

There was a terrible silence. 'Holy shit,' Lotte breathed.

He clamped his hands over his face and tried holding his breath.

Suddenly she was beside him and he felt her arm around him.

Another sob escaped him and he tried breathing in deeply.

'Was it Kyle and Brett?'

He couldn't reply.

'They're brainless dicks. I hate them, I really hate them,' Lotte said.

Raven sniffed hard, willing himself to stop crying.

'Kyle and Brett are so pathetic,' she went on vehemently. 'They just pick on anyone they're jealous of. They pick on Benny because he's top of the class, they pick on Carlos because he's brilliant at football, and they pick on you because you're good-looking and all the girls fancy you.'

He pressed his fingers firmly against his eyelids and sniffed hard. 'I don't give a fuck about Kyle and Brett,' he lied, trying to cover his embarrassment.

'What's the matter then?'

His mind groped for an excuse that might permit him to shed the role of pathetic victim.

'Is it about your mum?' Lotte suddenly asked, offering him a way out.

'Yes,' he said instantly. 'Yes.' After all, wasn't everything about his mum in the end?

'Is it true that she was murdered?' Lotte asked, her voice lowering to a reverent hush.

Raven dragged his fingers down his cheeks and looked at Lotte's wide brown eyes for the first time. 'Yeah. And I know who killed her.'

There was a silence. Lotte drew away and looked at

him for a long moment, studying his face carefully. Then she narrowed her eyes suspiciously. 'You're lying.'

'I'm not.'

She continued to look at him, her brow furrowed. Her pupils were very big, reflecting the light from above.

'Then you're joking. And that's not funny.'

'I'm not joking,' Raven said, wiping his cheeks with the sleeve of his blazer as the bus swung into view.

On the empty top deck Lotte sat down beside him. He could feel her eyes boring into the side of his head.

After several moments she said, 'Are you really telling me the truth?'

He nodded without looking round.

'How do you know?'

'I saw him. I was there.'

'Who was it?'

'Her boyfriend, Steve,' Raven said. 'They weren't getting on. He came round one day while she was cooking dinner and they had a massive row. He followed her out onto the balcony and pushed her over the rail.' The words burst from him as if with a force of their own. It was like a sudden release to be actually telling someone about it.

'But' – Lotte was still frowning – 'didn't someone see him do it? Didn't you tell the police? Why didn't they arrest him?'

'I did tell the police. Nobody believed me. Steve said it was an accident. He said she slipped and fell. And the police and everyone believed him. They just kept saying she'd had an accident.'

'But are you sure? Maybe it looked like he pushed her because they were arguing. But maybe she really did slip and fall.'

'Our balcony had a railing this high.' Raven held his hand out at waist height. 'You couldn't just fall off it. Steve told the police that she had been sitting on the edge of the railing and it had broken and she had fallen. But it's not true. Steve was mad at her. They were having a row. He grabbed her by her shirt, lifted her up and chucked her over the railing.'

Lotte was silent for a moment, her eyes narrowed. 'And the police believed Steve?'

'Yes.'

'And so he's just walking around, scot-free?'

'Yes, for the last two years.'

'D'you know where he lives?'

'I know where he used to live.'

Lotte stared at him, her eyes wide, shocked.

'What about your dad? Have you told him? Does he believe Steve's story too?'

'I never knew my dad,' Raven retorted. 'He buggered off before I was even born.'

Lotte was silent again drinking all this in. 'Don't you want to do something? Don't you want to try and get him caught? Don't you want to try and make him confess? You could go to his house. You could spy on him. You could get him drunk and trick him into confessing to you. Then someone could be filming secretly and you could show the tape to the police.'

Raven turned to look at her suddenly. 'You better not tell anyone about this. You better *swear*—'

'I swear, I swear!' Lotte said quickly.

He abruptly turned away again, shaking his head in disgust. 'How am I supposed to trust you? It'll be all over school tomorrow, just like with those fuckers Kyle and Brett.' He was suddenly furious with himself for confiding in her.

'I'm not going to tell anyone,' Lotte said quietly. But he didn't believe her.

For the next few days he waited – waited for something to happen. For Kyle and Brett to come up to him, making jokes about Sherlock Holmes. For the girls to start whispering and giggling in corners as he passed. But nothing did.

On Friday Lotte plonked herself down opposite him at lunch. 'Table's too crowded.' She nodded over to where she normally sat.

Raven said nothing, picking up his chips one by one and munching them slowly. He waited for her to bring up the subject of his mum. Instead she asked him whether he wanted to be her partner for the history project they had to do over half term.

He looked at her suspiciously. 'Mr Miles said it wasn't compulsory to do it in pairs.'

'Yes, but it'll be half the work if we do,' Lotte pointed out.

He supposed she was right. 'What are you doing it on?' he asked guardedly.

She rolled her eyes. 'I dunno. Henry the Eighth and all his blimmin' wives?'

Raven smiled slightly. 'Fine. What d'you want me to do?'

'You could come round to mine tomorrow. My brother's a history nut and we've got tons of books on Henry the Eighth lying around.'

'I'll have to ask,' Raven said.

'Cool.' She smiled, took out a pen and reached for a napkin. 'I'll give you my number.'

Raven snatched the napkin out of her hand. He wasn't falling for that one again. 'I'll give you mine,' he said instead.

'That's wonderful!' Jackie's whole face lit up when Raven told her that he would be going round to Lotte's the next day to work on a shared school project. 'Isn't Lotte that rather pretty girl who used to go to Ella's ballet school? Quite a character, I seem to remember. Gave up ballet for judo, I think. Remember, Dan, we met her parents last year at the Rosterfield summer ball.'

'Can't say I do.' Dan was busy unrolling some posters that he had bought on his way home from work. He held up one of Thierry Henry. 'What about this one?' he asked Raven.

Raven pretended to consider it for a moment before giving it a shake of the head.

'You must!' Jackie persisted. 'The mother does something in advertising. He's a sports journalist. You can't have forgotten!'

'I know Lotte,' Ella said. 'Is she your girlfriend now?'

'Ella!' Jackie exclaimed. 'You mustn't ask questions like that, young lady. Those things are private!'

'She's not even a friend,' Raven said quickly. 'She's

just a girl in my class who – who I have to do the history project with.'

'You should make her your girlfriend,' Ella said. 'She's nice.'

'Ella!'

'It's just a project,' Raven said.

Lotte opened the door to him wearing jeans and a grey sweatshirt and one red sock and led him through the maze of rollerblades and trainers that filled the hall. They went into the kitchen, where Lotte's brother, Tom, was ensconced with two friends and an assortment of pizza boxes and Coke cans. One boy sat by the half-open kitchen window, smoking a cigarette; the other was play-ing games on the computer. Tom sat with his feet up on the kitchen table, watching MTV.

Lotte went to the fridge and threw it open. Taking out some juice, she held it up enquiringly to Raven, who just had time to shake his head from the doorway before Tom looked up and said, 'Hey, it's my little sister and her boyfriend!'

The boy with the cigarette turned round and laughed.

'Shut up!' Lotte shouted, seizing an empty pizza box and hurling it at her brother's head.

Tom caught it with a grin.

'Isn't she a bit young?' the boy with the cigarette asked as Lotte started going through the pizza boxes on the table and wailing, 'You haven't left any for me!'

'Here. Take this and shut up,' Tom said, handing her a box. 'You can share it with your boyfriend.'

They started to laugh again and Raven backed out into the corridor.

'Sorry about that,' Lotte said when they had retreated to the safety of her bedroom with half a pizza and a carton of juice and two cups. 'Tom thinks he's so entertaining.'

She closed the bedroom door firmly behind them and Raven gave an embarrassed shrug as they sat down, cross-legged, on her sheepskin rug among a pile of stuffed animals. He couldn't believe how messy her room was: the carpet was almost entirely hidden by clothes.

She handed him a large slice of pizza and they started to eat.

'Hey,' Lotte said suddenly. 'What's that on your arm?'

Munching, Raven glanced down. A small red patch of blood was slowly soaking into the sleeve of his pale sweatshirt.

'Look,' Lotte said. 'You're bleeding.'

Raven gave it a dismissive rub.

'What happened? Let's see.'

'It's nothing,' Raven replied quickly.

'It's not nothing. It's blood—'

'It's just a scab that came off.'

'Oh.' Lotte reached up to haul a hefty tome off her desk.

'I figured we could do it in two parts,' she said. 'I'll do the boring part, if you like, about his parents and when he was born and how he grew up, and you can do the interesting part about how he bumped off all his wives—' She froze suddenly.

Raven glanced at her, surprised. 'What?'

Lotte looked faintly horrified. 'I didn't mean— Shit, perhaps you'd rather do the first half . . .'

He shrugged. 'I don't care which half I do.'

'Are – are you sure?' Lotte seemed flustered. 'Because I don't mind which bit I do either, so – so I may as well do the second half since – since, you know—'

She broke off. Raven regarded her steadily over the pile of books on the carpet. Lotte was hunting about among the clothing strewn around her for a pen, her cheeks flushed with embarrassment.

Raven took a deep breath. 'You know, I *am* going to get justice for her,' he said quietly.

Lotte carried on hunting for a moment, so that he wasn't sure she had actually heard him. But then she stopped and glanced up at him nervously.

'Really? How?'

'D'you want to help me?' He kept his voice steady, but suddenly his heart was in his mouth.

Lotte took a deep breath and exhaled slowly. Her eyes did not leave his. 'We'd have to think of a really good plan—' she began.

'I've got a plan,' Raven said quickly. 'But I can only trust you with it if you're in.'

Lotte stared at him, chewing her lower lip, but there was a glint of excitement in her eyes.

Raven sat back. 'Never mind.' He flicked open a book. 'So where exactly am I starting from? The wedding in fifteen-oh-nine to Catherine of Aragon?'

'Wait.' Lotte touched his hand, then withdrew abruptly. 'I'll help you. I'm in. Tell me your plan.'

He slowly lifted his eyes from the book. 'Are you sure?'

She nodded, her eyes very wide.

Raven snapped the book shut and knelt up on the carpet. 'OK. Listen. If you want someone to tell you a secret, there are basically two ways of going about it. One is to befriend them and get them to trust you, so that they want to confide in you. The other is to scare the shit out of them.'

Lotte stared at him. 'And which one are you going to try?'

'I don't know yet. Maybe I'll try both. But that's why I need a second person. I think I know a way of tricking Steve into confiding in me. But I'd need the other person to be secretly filming him so that afterwards we could give the tape to the police—'

'But how are you going to get him to confess?' Lotte looked sceptical. 'And how am I going to film him without him noticing?'

'We'd need to start off by checking if he's still living in the same place in Hounslow,' Raven said steadily. 'Then we'll need to follow him around a bit to find out as much information about him as possible – like if he's got a girlfriend, what he does for a living, stuff like that. Once we know all that, we can devise a proper plan.'

'And how are we going to film it if we *do* manage to get him to confess?' Lotte asked.

'Easy,' Raven said. 'My foster dad's got one of those palm-sized camcorders. If we do it right, Steve will never even know.'

Lotte nodded slowly, thoughtfully. 'When do we start?'

'On Monday. I'm going to say that I'm staying late after school to work in the library.'

Lotte nodded. 'OK, I'll do the same.'

'Then I'll meet you outside the tube station straight

after last period. We'll take the tube to Hounslow and I'll show you where he lives, OK?'

'OK,' Lotte echoed quietly. But her eyes were bright.

He caught Lotte's eye as he came into class on Monday morning and she gave him the thumbs-up sign quickly before sitting down. The day seemed to go on for ever, and by three thirty his nerves felt raw. As soon as the last bell went, he grabbed his things and headed quickly towards the underground.

Lotte was waiting inside, her blue scarf wound tightly round her neck, her bare knees below her too-short school skirt bright pink from the cold.

They bought tickets from the machine and followed the steady stream of passengers down onto the train. At Hounslow Central they emerged into the darkened high street, its pavement still littered with empty crates and rubbish where the market had stood during the day. Raven walked fast, hands dug deep into his pockets, leading Lotte down past the fire station and over the road towards Easton Street, to number forty-nine, where Steve used to live. Several of the houses in the street were boarded up now.

Lotte looked around anxiously. 'God, does anyone actually live here?'

'I know, it's a real shithole,' Raven said. 'But look, that's Steve's flat. It looks like someone still lives there!'

Two windows were lit on the third floor. That was a start. Leaving Lotte glancing nervously up and down the lamplit street, Raven took the steps up to the front door two at a time, and hurriedly scanned the buzzers... WINCHAM. The ink was smudged and fading, but the name was still recognizable. His heart began to thump as he rejoined Lotte on the other side of the road, peering up at the curtained windows.

'He still lives here,' Raven whispered in her ear.

'Do you think he's in there now?' Lotte's breath made a small cloud of white smoke around her mouth as she talked.

'I don't know.' Raven pulled up the sleeve of his coat to look at his watch. 'It's only half past four. Maybe he's still at work.'

'Is he married?'

'He wasn't when I knew him. He lived on his own. Mum and I would come here all the time.'

'Well, somebody's in there, unless they've left the light on.'

'I'm going to ring the bell,' Raven said, suddenly decisive.

'Wait, wait.' Lotte clutched at his arm. 'Won't he

recognize you? Then he might smell a rat, figure that we've come to shop him to the police or something. He might pack up and disappear and—'

'He has no idea that I know. He came to her funeral, for Christ's sake. He thought I was in bed asleep when he pushed her. He thought I only woke up when I heard her scream.'

But Lotte didn't let go of his sleeve. 'What are you going to say then?' she whispered. 'Isn't he going to think it a bit weird, you just turning up out of the blue to see him?'

Raven stopped and thought. 'I can pretend I'm looking for something,' he began. 'Something – I dunno – something that belonged to my mum. I know: the dolphin necklace she always wore. I've got it at home but I can pretend I haven't. I can pretend I thought the police gave it to him.'

'OK . . .' Lotte swallowed. She looked nervous suddenly, her eyes wide and unblinking.

'You can stay here if you like, or wait for me at the end of the street,' Raven said. 'I won't be long. He'll probably just say, "No, bugger off," and I'll have to leave, but at least I may get a chance to see if he's still living alone.'

Lotte breathed deeply. 'No, I said I'd help,' she said. 'I'm coming in with you. Besides, I really need to use the toilet. Do you think he'd let me use his toilet?'

'Probably. Hey, that could help us. I could keep him talking and you could have a quick look around his flat. See if you can pick up any clues.'

'What sort of clues?' Lotte looked worried.

'Anything. Like a name on a letter. Try and see if he's married or where he works.'

'I can have a go,' Lotte said dubiously.

'OK,' Raven said. 'Let's do it!'

Raven pressed the buzzer long and hard. He glanced at Lotte. She was smiling at him nervously and sort of jiggling about a bit, obviously desperate to pee.

'There's no one there!' Lotte whispered, turning round to go back down the steps.

'Wait!' Raven grabbed her arm.

Suddenly there was a crackling on the intercom and then a man's voice. 'Yes? Hello?'

Lotte gasped, clapping a gloved hand to her mouth.

Raven squeezed her hand hard to shush her and then spoke into the intercom. 'Is that Steve?'

Lotte gasped again and started hopping up and down, whether from nerves or the urge to pee, Raven couldn't tell.

There was a silence from the intercom. Then, 'Hold on, I'll be right down.'

Raven stepped back from the door and looked at

Lotte. Suddenly it was hard to breathe. Lotte was biting her thumb, looking at him with an agonized expression, which didn't help. They both stood there, frozen, until there was the sound of footsteps from inside and the door opened halfway, revealing a thinnish, balding man in a grey tracksuit and slippers.

'Steve,' Raven said quietly.

Steve gazed down at them, his eyes widening. 'Raven! What on earth—? Well, this is a huge surprise!'

Raven felt his jaw tighten. 'I've just come to ask you something.'

'Crikey, you've grown! And who's this?'

Lotte stared.

'Lotte,' Raven said. 'A friend from school.'

'Oh . . . I see . . .' Steve looked puzzled. He glanced behind them, up and down the pavement. 'Does the social worker know you're here?'

'Yeah,' Raven lied. 'I'm looking for something. Something that belonged to Mum. I thought you might—'

'Raven' – Steve's voice was gentle, almost patronizing – 'come on, we've talked about this. You know I haven't kept anything . . . Look, come in, let's talk about it.'

They followed him up a narrow, carpetless staircase and in through a yellow door to his flat. Junk mail still littered the floor and there was a strong smell of onions.

They followed Steve into a small, untidy living room and sat side by side on the sagging brown couch. Steve perched on the edge of the armchair, clasping and unclasping his hands, looking nervous. 'I'm afraid I can't offer you much. If you'd told me you were coming . . .'

'That's all right,' Lotte said.

Steve sat back and looked at Raven. 'You've grown,' he said again. 'Those new folks looking after you properly, are they?'

'Yeah,' Raven answered.

There was an awkward silence. 'How's school?' Steve asked.

Raven shrugged.

'Look, son,' Steve said suddenly, 'I wish I could give you something of your mum's but the truth is, I didn't keep any of her stuff.'

Raven was aware of a faint prickling in his eyes. 'What, you just threw it all away?'

Steve cleared his throat awkwardly. 'Raven, we've all moved on—'

Raven felt his chest tighten and he glared at Steve. 'Do I look like I've moved on?'

Suddenly he felt Lotte's foot pressing urgently against his. 'Um, excuse me, Mr, uh . . .'

'Just Steve.'

'Steve, can I use your bathroom? It's just that we had quite a long journey here, and . . .'

Steve smiled sympathetically. 'Sure. Last door on the right.'

Lotte got up and went out, shooting a wide-eyed look over her shoulder as she left. Raven kept his head turned away from Steve, fixing on a dirty spot on the wall. There was a silence.

'Look, Raven, what's going on here? The social worker doesn't know, does she?'

Raven said nothing, staring hard at the wall.

'He's got a kid,' was the first thing Lotte said when they emerged back onto the frosty, lamplit street.

Raven said nothing. They were walking fast, breathing hard, hurrying back to the warmth and relative familiarity of the tube station.

'He's got a kid,' Lotte repeated. 'There were bath toys and a messy kid's bedroom. Raven, are you listening?'

'Yeah, yeah.'

'At least we found what we were looking for. At least we know he's still in the same flat, like a sitting duck, with no idea anyone knows his secret.'

'Mm.'

'Aren't you interested?' Lotte sounded peeved. 'Did you even know he had a kid?'

'No—'

'Well, maybe the kid wasn't there because it lives half the time with its mum or something. Maybe we could find out some information about Steve on the Internet. Wincham is a fairly unusual name. We could Google him. I've done it before. It's easy. You just type in the name *Steve Wincham* between quotation marks, and *any* record of that exact name comes up, even if it's just like the members' list of a sports club or something.'

After a while Lotte gave up talking and they rode the tube home in silence. Raven sat unmoving, staring out of the black windows.

'This is my stop,' Lotte said as they rattled into Gunnersbury. 'I'll see you tomorrow, OK?'

He didn't even look at her as she got up and stepped out of the carriage, the sliding doors banging closed behind her.

Chapter Six

The following week was half term and Lotte was away visiting her grandparents, so there was no opportunity to take the plan further. Raven resisted offers of board games and ignored interruptions from Ella as much as he could, and spent most of the time devouring the book Lotte had given him. He was in the middle of a really thrilling bit when he was startled by a knock on his bedroom door. It was Dan. 'We thought we'd go for a walk in the park since it's so sunny and maybe kick a ball around,' he said. 'Coming?'

Raven looked at him stonily. 'Do I have to?'

'Come on, it'll do us all good to get out,' Dan replied.

Raven got wearily off his bed and started hunting around for his outdoor things. It was freezing out and the sun was a harsh icy light in a bright blue sky.

Richmond Park was almost deserted but breathtakingly beautiful, a thin powdering of snow on the ground, the deer grazing peacefully on the few remaining patches of green grass. Ella tried to creep up to them, her pink scarf trailing in the snow behind her. Dan started a game of football, laying out sticks as goalposts. Ella soon tired of the skittish deer and joined in, screeching, 'Me, me, me!' whenever someone else had the ball. Dan kicked the ball over to Raven but he rolled it back and turned away and climbed onto an enormous fallen tree trunk that looked down over a lake. The icy air stung against his lips; his warm breath evaporated into white smoke that rose into the trees. The cold seeped through his gloves and deep into his fingers, through his beanie and into his ears, through his scarf and into his neck, through his coat and into his stomach. If he stayed here long enough, he would freeze to death. How did the deer manage? Did they not feel the cold at all through their coats of fur? We humans are so defenceless compared to the rest of the natural world, he thought to himself. We have no shell to protect us, no fur, no horns, no claws. We are just soft skin and fragile bones; we have only our minds to figure out a way to keep ourselves safe, and sometimes that's just not enough. We can be so easily hurt, so easily broken, so easily damaged beyond repair.

There was a scrabbling noise behind him. He turned his head. Dan was pulling himself up onto the tree trunk beside him, panting from the game, his cheeks flushed pink from the cold and exertion. 'Hey, buddy.'

Raven nodded and stared back towards the treetops in the distance, their branches lit up by the winter sun. Jackie and Ella's voices rang out as they continued their game – squawks of laughter, gasps and pants. 'D'you want to come and join in?' Dan asked him.

He shook his head, his eyes fixed on the misty horizon.

'Buddy, what's on your mind?' Dan asked after a couple of minutes of silence.

Raven felt a small pain start at the back of his throat. He didn't move. He felt a hand on his shoulder. 'Tell me,' Dan said.

His face suddenly felt very hot. He said nothing.

'Maybe I could help,' Dan said quietly. 'Won't you give me a try?'

For a split second Raven considered it. He actually considered confiding to Dan what Steve had done. He considered telling Dan about Kyle and Brett and how they were making his life hell. About how alone he felt, about how every day hurt. Then he remembered who Dan was. His foster parent. His paid-by-the-state-to-look-after-somebody-else's-kid-in-order-to-make-you-feel-good-about-yourself foster parent. And so he shook his head.

'Sometimes talking about things can help,' Dan said.

The pain in his throat intensified and there was a sharp pricking in his eyes. He clenched his jaw, willing the tears not to fall.

'You must miss her so much,' Dan said quietly. He put his arm round Raven's shoulders, and in silence they continued watching the deer.

Lotte was shooting meaningful looks at him across the classroom on Monday. He had arrived ten minutes after the bell, minus his blazer, and had already been told off for being late, and for not wearing his blazer. There had been a scene in the car involving Ella and a doll called Annabel and the air still seemed to reverberate with Ella's wails. As he sat down, still gasping from having run up four flights of stairs, he noticed Lotte, eyebrows raised, mouthing something. He frowned at her, then spread out his hands to indicate that he didn't understand, when Mr Rumbold said, 'Lotte, if you could possibly prise your eyes away from the back of the class and glance at what's going on at the front . . .' And so that was the end of that.

At first break Kyle and Brett were buzzing around him

like a couple of flies and so he stayed well clear of Lotte, but then, at the end of break, Alice came up to him and shoved something into his hand, whispering, 'Lotte said to give you this.'

Then the bell rang, so there was no time to look at it, but during geography he unfolded the piece of paper slowly, carefully, just under the edge of his desk. Then, when the teacher was looking away, he glanced down at it as it lay on his lap. It was a printout from the Internet, entitled *Hounslow Post Online*. Beneath the heading SPORTS DAY AT PARKSIDE PRIMARY SCHOOL was a caption circled in red: *Billy Wincham and his dad, Steve Wincham, were the proud winners of the parent–pupil relay race.* A small boy with a wide grin stood proudly holding out his medal. And by his side was Steve.

He felt himself freeze. His heart began to hammer and a painful lump rose in his throat. He stared hard at the grainy photograph. Steve was beaming proudly, his arm round his son. *His son.* Light-headed with shock, Raven looked over at Lotte but she actually seemed to be paying attention for a change and all he could see was the back of her head. How had she found this?

He waited until Kyle and Brett were engaged in a game of football at the bottom of the playground before approaching Lotte.

'Clever, aren't I?' she said.

'How did you find it?'

'I did exactly what I said I'd do. Typed *Steve Wincham* into Google and looked to see what it found. Only one entry for Steve Wincham came up, and when I clicked on the link and saw his picture, I recognized him instantly. And I managed to look up the kid's school address as well.'

Raven felt the page in his hand begin to shake.

'I can't believe he's got a son,' Lotte said. 'He looks so cute. How old is he, d'you reckon?'

'Five,' Raven said.

Lotte suddenly looked at him more closely. 'Did you know Steve had a son?'

'No.'

Lotte chewed her lower lip thoughtfully. 'If Steve didn't want you and your mum to know about his son, then that must have been because— Oh my God!' She clapped a hand to her mouth.

Raven looked sharply at her. 'What?'

'I've got it! Steve must have still been married to some other woman! Maybe he wasn't divorced then. He had a kid with her, this Billy, and meanwhile was cheating on his wife with your mum!'

'But we don't know—'

'Yes, listen, it all makes sense. If Steve was two-timing your mum and Billy's mum, maybe your mum found out and threatened to tell Billy's mum, and so Steve went mad and pushed your mum off the balcony!'

Raven continued to stare at her. 'What?' he repeated dumbly.

'Yes, yes! It all makes sense!' Lotte was hopping up and down. 'He was cheating on Billy's mum by seeing your mum. Then your mum got mad and was going to break up with him and tell Billy's mum. Steve didn't want to lose both of them and so he pushed *your* mum off the balcony to shut her up. For good,' she added for emphasis.

Raven exhaled slowly. 'OK . . .'

'Yes, it makes perfect sense. Can't you remember what they were arguing about? Can't you remember anything at all?'

Raven shook his head. He suddenly felt very tired.

'Say something, Raven. You look really strange,' Lotte said.

Raven sat down on the damp asphalt beside the wall and brought his knees up to his chest.

'Are you OK? You've gone really pale.' Lotte's eyes were close up and peering.

'I'm OK,' Raven said in an uneven voice. He bit the

side of his thumb, hard, and wondered if he was going to
be sick.

'I mean, I might be wrong,' Lotte said suddenly.
'Maybe – maybe it's not that at all—' She broke off as the
bell began to ring.

Raven got to his feet and took a deep breath. 'Well,
we'll just have to find out,' he said as they set off for their
classroom.

'How?' Lotte persisted.

'I'll think of something.'

'Think of something now!' she urged him. 'Come on,
come on, this could be our clue!'

Raven stopped walking so suddenly that Lotte
bumped into him. They were halfway up the empty
playground and the last of the pupils were disappearing
into the entrance ahead.

'The bell went five minutes ago! Get a move on!' Mr
Rumbold shouted at them.

Lotte hesitated, looking at Raven. 'What's the matter?'

'We'll have to skip school,' he said.

Lotte looked shocked. 'What? Why?'

'Tomorrow, after lunch. We have to skip school after
lunch. If we leave here at two, we can be at Billy's school
before three thirty. We can see who picks him up.'

'What if it's his mum?'

'Are you two deaf? I said, get a move on!' Mr Rumbold yelled from the top of the playground.

'Quick!' Raven said. 'We won't be able to talk later. I'll meet you tomorrow at the end of lunch break outside the music room in the basement. We can wait till the playground is clear and then climb over the gates—'

'I'm not sure, Raven . . .' Lotte's brown eyes were anxious. 'If we get caught, we'll be in deep shit—'

'*Inside! Now!*'

'As long as nobody sees us sneak out, we won't get caught,' Raven said. 'Tomorrow afternoon is perfect. It's double art and Mrs Doherty never remembers to take the register.'

Still Lotte hesitated. 'Kyle and Brett . . .'

'Even they won't want to be branded a grass.'

'*If I have to call you one more time . . .!*' Mr Rumbold roared.

Raven grabbed her by the wrist. 'Are you in or are you out?'

'OK, I'll do it!' Lotte gave a nervous, breathless laugh and they both broke into a run.

That evening, after school, he was staring out of the window, watching a large pigeon sitting on a bare wet branch, when there was a knock on the door. He ignored it. The knocking continued. Faint but very persistent. He got up and opened the door.

Ella stood there, holding something that looked like a cross between a rabbit and a kangaroo. 'Do you want to play with me?'

'No,' Raven said.

She put her finger in her mouth and frowned. 'Why?'

'Because I don't like the same games as five-year-old girls.'

'So?' Ella challenged him. 'Maybe I like the same games as fourteen-year-old boys!'

'Like what for example?'

Ella thought for a minute. 'Cars?' she suggested hopefully.

'Nope.'

She thought again, frowning hard. 'Trains?'

'Nope.'

'War games?'

'Nope.'

'Superman and Supergirl?'

'Look, Ella, I can't play with you now, I'm busy.'

'Busy doing what?'

'Something.'

'I don't believe you. You're just sitting there, doing nothing. You never play with me and you never come and see me at lunch break any more, too.'

'Go and ask your mummy to entertain you.'

Ella pouted. 'She keeps saying she's busy. She's too busy arguing with Daddy about you.'

Raven looked at her. 'What?'

'They're in the kitchen talking about you and they said I have to go upstairs to my room and entertain myself for a while. I don't *want* to entertain myself for a while!'

'OK,' Raven said quickly. 'I've got a game. It's called eavesdropping. You have to sit very quietly on the stairs and see who has the best hearing. We have to try and hear everything that's being said in the kitchen.'

Ella's eyes widened. 'Ooh, I've got very good hearing,' she said proudly.

'Good. Come on then.'

They crept halfway down the stairs and sat on the middle step. Ella leaned forward, chin on her knees, a frown of concentration on her face. Raven chewed his thumbnail.

'I'm trying, Dan.' Jackie's voice sounded tired. 'I'm trying. But it doesn't seem to make any difference.'

'Well, we have to keep on trying.' Dan's voice now. 'We can't give up. That's what he wants. That's what he *expects*. If we give up, then we just fit into the mould of all the other adults in his life who've abandoned him.'

'But I feel like we're beating our heads against a brick wall. Nothing we say or do makes any difference. He's still as monosyllabic as the first day he arrived!' Jackie sounded angry.

'Come on, that's not true,' Dan said. 'There have been some improvements. He actually answers our questions now instead of just shrugging. And he seems to have made a friend at school—'

'He won't even look at me,' Jackie interrupted him. 'It's like we're not even people to him. Just givers of food and shelter—'

'But that's just what we are, Jackie! We're not his parents, we can't expect him to love us, or need us. He won't let himself get attached to us because, as far as he's concerned, we could disappear tomorrow and he could be on to his next foster family.'

'Well, maybe' – Jackie's voice wavered – 'maybe another family would be able to get through to him and make a relationship with him—'

'You're not thinking of giving up already?'

'I'm just tired, Dan! When we decided to take the plunge and have a go at fostering, we never thought we'd be landed with a teenager – much less a disturbed one. We were thinking of a playmate for Ella, because we couldn't have any more children, because we didn't want her to be an only child—'

'He's not disturbed, Jackie. Just bereaved.'

'There are spots of blood on his school shirts, Dan. Have you seen his arms lately? It's just getting worse! And it's like he's carved out of stone – there's no reaction, no emotion, no anything! It's so draining – it's just take, take, take, there's nothing in return—'

'We can't expect him to be grateful—'

'Not grateful, just – I don't know – something! Just an acknowledgement that we exist would be nice!'

'Raven, Raven, wait for me!'

Ella's voice reached him over the slap of his trainers against the pavement and the pounding of his heart in his chest, but he didn't slow down. He turned the corner, raced across the road and kept on going, past the old ladies at the bus stop, past the supermarket and pet store, up to the end of the road and beyond. Suddenly the hard concrete beneath his feet was replaced by soft grass – he reached the common and overtook a solitary jogger, a couple walking their dog. The grass grew longer, the dark shadows of trees greeted him ahead. He ran between them and slowed to a gasping halt, one hand on the tree trunk, doubled over, trying to catch his breath. Red heat pulsated in front of his eyes. He lowered himself to his knees on the damp, pungent earth, took out his penknife and pressed it against the soft white flesh of his arm. The sudden silver shaft of pain took his breath away, making him gasp. As he pressed down with his fingers on either side of the gash, making the warm blood trickle down his arm and over his wrist and down between his fingers, the cut began to throb, painfully, reassuringly. He let his head fall to his knees. The sobs, when they came, were thick, fast and furious, tearing at his throat, pulling huge hot tears from his eyes. He pressed his forehead against the coarse lined bark of the tree and felt his knees sink gently into the damp-smelling earth, his tears soaking his hands, running in warm bloody rivulets between his fingers and down his wrists . . . It was a long time before he could stop. After a while his throat began to hurt and his shoulders to ache and he sat down on the ground, leaning against the tree . . . and saw Ella standing there, watching him.

He took a deep, ragged breath. 'Go away!' he shouted.

Ella didn't move, her eyes wide.

'Go home!' Raven shouted again. 'Go back to your mummy and daddy!'

'I can't,' Ella said soberly. 'I've lost myself.'

'Then just go away and leave me alone!'

'It's too dangerous,' she said. 'Someone might take me. You're my brother. You have to look after me.'

'What makes you think I can keep you safe? Maybe I'm crazy! Maybe I'm dangerous!'

'You're not dangerous, you're my brother,' Ella said again.

'I'm not your fucking brother!' Raven shouted.

'You shouldn't say the F word,' she chided him. 'And anyway, you're my *foster* brother.'

'I'm not your anything! Go away!'

'I picked you some flowers.' Ella held out a tiny bunch of wilting snowdrops. 'I picked you some flowers to make you feel better.'

'I don't want your stupid flowers!'

She ignored him and laid the tiny bunch on the ground beside him. 'D'you wanna play hide and seek?'

She sat down cross-legged in the grass beside him and held out her stuffed animal. 'Do you want Roo? You can have Roo if you want. Here.'

'I d-don't want your stupid rabbit!' he sobbed, turning his back to her.

'He's not a rabbit, silly, he's a kangaroo! He's called Roo – that's short for kangaroo! Look, he's got a pouch and pointy ears and a long tail. Rabbits don't have a

pouch and pointy ears and a long tail!' She waved the
stuffed animal in front of his face, then, when he didn't
respond, nuzzled it softly against his cheek. 'Ooh, ooh,
I'm Roo! I'm a kangaroo, not a rabbit!' she said in a high
voice.

'Get off—'

'Ooh, ooh, I'm Roo! Look at me – am I a rabbit or a
kangaroo?'

Raven sniffed hard and wiped his hand across his
face. 'You're a rabbit, you silly animal,' he said.

'Ooh, ooh, I'm Roo! Is Roo short for rabbit or
kangaroo?'

'You're only called Roo because your owner doesn't
know what a kangaroo looks like.'

'Ooh, ooh, I'm Roo! My owner is not silly, she's the
second cleverest in her whole class!'

'Your owner's a show-off.'

'No she's not – it's not her fault if she's clever! Don't
you think she's clever?'

Raven took a shaky breath. 'I suppose she's fairly
clever for a five-year-old. But she's a show-off too.'

Ella stuck her tongue out at him and then started to
laugh.

He got to his feet. 'We'd better go back,' he said quietly.
'Before your parents send out a search party for you.'

Ella got up reluctantly. 'But I want to play,' she protested.

He took her hand. 'OK. Here's a game. We have to get home without walking on any of the cracks in the pavement. The first one to step on a crack is the loser.'

By lunch time the next day his heart was thudding. OK, so today he really had a reason to keep an eye on the time. At a quarter to two, ten minutes before the bell, he had to find a way of slipping, unnoticed, back into the school building. He had to hope that Lotte would get away successfully too. Then they would meet in the basement, outside the music room, and wait – wait until the bell went, wait until the school stampede had died down before slipping, again hopefully unnoticed, across the playground, up and over the locked gates and into the street.

At half past one Raven stood by the fence, at a spot where it was easy to see the teacher on duty, and tried to look inconspicuous, his hands in his pockets. Laura, a redhead from his class who often seemed to end up sitting next to him, had a stab at engaging him in conversation, but when all she got was a couple of monosyllabic replies, she soon melted away. Lotte was over by the wall with Alice, chatting to her so animatedly and ignoring him so completely that he began to fear she had forgotten. Kyle and Brett had started off their break by gate-crashing a game of basketball. After some of the boys had gone over to Mrs Harrison to complain and Kyle and Brett had got shouted at and banned from the basketball area, they had tried skimming stones across a large puddle of water, rapidly progressing to throwing stones at some of the Year Seven boys who inadvertently got in their way. They had then gone on to a game of jumping-in-puddles-and-splashing-the-girls, but the girls in question quickly moved off to a dryer part of the play-ground and Raven realized that Kyle and Brett were beginning to get bored.

Brett had a go first, charging at him from a distance, pretending for Mrs Harrison's benefit that it was a complete accident and even managing a 'Whoops, sorry,' as he crashed into Raven from behind. Raven staggered and only just managed not to fall, but Brett had timed it nicely with Mrs Harrison turning her head to look at two boys arguing by the wall so she didn't notice. Next was Kyle, creeping up on him from behind and kicking him in the back of the knee so that his leg buckled. When Raven turned round, he saw that Lotte had gone from the wall and, in her place, Alice was talking to another girl, Sonia. Then Kyle head-butted him in the side as

Mrs Harrison went over to sort out the two arguing boys, and as Raven straightened up from that, winded, he saw that it was nearly two o'clock.

A feeling of panic began to rise. Once Mrs Harrison rang the bell it would be too late: the pupils would begin to line up in the playground and Mrs Harrison would be in front of the school doors, bellowing at the stragglers at the end of the playground and sending the prefects to check the toilets. Raven would have to get into line with his class, no doubt with Kyle and Brett right behind him, and there would be no further chance to slip away during the quick-march straight up to class. Lotte would have hidden in vain: she would wait for him and wait for him and he would never come, and what would she think of him then? No, this was his only chance – he had to do something, and quickly.

Mrs Harrison was moving away from the squabbling boys, checking her watch and drifting closer and closer to the playground bell. Kyle and Brett were getting their last laughs of the afternoon break, pretending to be running races with each other but making absolutely sure that Raven got in their way. It was getting desperate: the school clock read five minutes to, and Mrs Harrison was heading towards the bell. He was going to have to act, and act now. Kyle was running towards him again, ready for another 'accidental' shove. Out of the corner of his eye, Raven watched him like a hawk, and then, just as Kyle lurched in towards him, he threw himself against Kyle. They smacked into each other hard, Raven's shoulder making contact with Kyle's chest. The jolt of pain took his breath away. With a blood-curdling yell, Kyle collapsed in a heap, clutching his chest and gasping dramatically. Raven staggered back, gripping his shoulder and groaning. He was aware that Mrs Harrison had dropped her hand from the bell rope.

'Miss, miss, he shoved into me on purpose!' Kyle was yelling, his face puce as the teacher strode towards them.

'Kyle Jones, you were the one running around like a demented bull,' Mrs Harrison snapped. 'Come on, try and stand up. Where are you hurt? Do you need to see the nurse?'

'Miss, I can't breathe! I can't breathe!' Kyle was shouting.

'Oh, for heaven's sake, calm down. Stand up, will you? Raven, go and ring the bell.'

It was his chance and he took it. Leaving Mrs Harrison standing over the still-gasping Kyle, he ran across to the top of the playground, gave the bell rope a hard shake and then darted round the side of the building, running down the stone steps to the basement door.

In the musty-smelling corridor the dimly lit walls seemed to echo with his rasping breath and his shoulder throbbed painfully. Lotte was standing obediently outside the music room, her hood pulled up and her school bag between her feet.

'I thought you weren't coming – I've been stressed out of my—!'

'Shh, shh!'

She grabbed his arm, her fingers digging into him. 'The bell's just gone – you nearly didn't make it! How long shall we wait? Somebody could come down here—'

'Five minutes,' Raven said breathlessly. 'The best time to go is when all the teachers are in class taking the register. Trust me, I've done it before.' He pulled up his sleeve and stared down at his watch, chewing his lower lip nervously. The sound of Lotte's voice was replaced by the thudding of his own heart.

'They'll be in class by now,' Lotte whispered, her eyes frantic. 'We should go!'

'One more minute,' Raven said, trying to slow his breathing. He knew he had to time this right. They had to make it work. If a teacher caught them, there would be hell to pay. Lotte would be in trouble and it would all be his fault. Dan and Jackie would be hauled up in front of the headmaster and it might be the last straw.

They would tell Joyce that they didn't want him any more, and he'd be sent back, back to Bedford House, or moved on to a new family . . . Not that he cared, of course, but Ella would be so upset.

Lotte covered her mouth with her gloved hand and began dancing from foot to foot.

'OK, now! Follow me! Quietly!'

They tiptoed up the stairs. On the ground-floor landing they stopped, holding their breaths, straining their ears for the sound of voices or footsteps. There was a distant clatter of chairs and a door slamming from the floor above. The faraway sound of a teacher shouting. But that was all. Raven turned his head to stare at Lotte. She looked as if she might burst.

'Follow me quickly to the doors when I say so,' he whispered. 'As soon as we reach the playground, run like mad. That way we'll be there for the shortest time possible, so if a teacher looks out of the window and sees us—'

'OK, OK,' Lotte whispered impatiently in return.

Raven turned back to face the front. One more careful listen for the sound of a loitering teacher. Nothing. 'Go,' he whispered.

Raven walked quickly to the double doors, praying Lotte was keeping close behind. His legs felt stiff and jerky from the desire to run. As the cold air met his face, he stopped to check for Lotte and she bumped right into him. There was a muffled squawk and then they were running, running, running, as hard and as fast as they could, towards the wrought-iron gate, their ears burning from the shout that they were convinced would follow them. Suddenly they had reached the gate, grasping the iron grating, reaching up as high as possible and scrabbling for a toe-hold. Raven was about to swing his leg over the top when he heard a gasp from below. 'Oh help, I can't—!'

He jumped back down into the playground again, his feet burning from the hefty drop. 'Take your school bag off, chuck it over, chuck it quick!' he gasped. 'Now put your foot in my hands – that's it, push up, push up! Now pull yourself over!' Suddenly Lotte swung herself over and jumped down onto the pavement. Raven quickly began to climb again.

They had been there too long: he was sure someone was going to start shouting soon – probably just as he straddled the very top of the gate – but to his amazement all remained quiet and he jumped down the other side, almost sending Lotte flying into the road. When they had both straightened up and recovered their bags, they saw that several passers-by had stopped on the other side of the street but they just laughed in euphoria and legged it to the tube station.

Safely inside the moving carriage, they were crazy with relief, laughing hysterically, momentarily trying to stop themselves as the other passengers looked at them in bemusement, then bursting out into laughter all over again.

'I nearly had a heart attack! I thought you were going to leave me behind – the gate was all wet and my foot kept slipping—!'

'I was almost at the top and then I looked down and you were still on the ground, and when I jumped down, I thought, What if I can't get you over? and then I was *sure* someone had seen us—!'

'I kept thinking, What if we get caught now, how could we talk ourselves out of it? Raven, I can't believe you made me do this!'

Gradually they calmed down, their mirth shrinking into short bursts whenever they caught each other's eye, and a sort of sleepiness began to set in, a kind of post-adrenaline exhaustion. When they got off at Hounslow, Billy Wincham was on Raven's mind again, and Lotte's laughter had faded.

With the help of Lotte's *A to Z*, they found Parkside School at the end of the high street, not far from the station. And then all they had to do was wait.

Gradually a small gaggle of mums and pushchairs began to gather around the painted red gate.

'We'll have to stay here,' Raven said from their position in the bus shelter across the road. 'If Steve sees us, we'll be in trouble.'

'But what if we can't recognize Billy from this distance?' Lotte asked.

'We'll just have to do our best – we can't risk bumping into them,' Raven countered.

They stood there in silence. Lotte was fiddling with her scarf; Raven was chewing his thumbnail. When the red gate suddenly opened, they both started.

Children began to trickle out. Small, stout children muffled up in coats and hats and scarves and gloves. Lotte groaned softly. 'They all look exactly the same . . .'

Children were being lifted up, hugged, kissed, bundled into buggies. Some mums moved off, more arrived. Suddenly Raven stiffened. A man had walked up and stopped at the gate. A man with a shabby denim jacket, narrow shoulders and a balding head. 'It's Steve,' he whispered.

'Where? Are you sure?'

'Yes. Shh.' Raven grabbed her hand. 'Watch out, he's going. Quick, let's follow him!'

Steve was easy to follow. The little boy didn't walk very fast and seemed to be talking a lot to his father. They turned off the high street, stopped to post a letter, then to pick up a fallen leaf, and turned into Steve's street. But as they drew level with Steve's building, they continued walking. Lotte grabbed hold of Raven's sleeve. 'What are they doing?' she whispered.

'There's a park at the end of the road – I think they're going there,' Raven said.

As predicted, Steve and Billy went through the park gates. Steve let go of Billy's hand and Billy broke into a run, heading straight for the playground. Steve lengthened his stride.

'Careful.' Lotte grabbed Raven's hand as they approached the low wooden frame that surrounded the swings and climbing frame. 'He'll catch sight of us.'

They drew back into the shadow of the trees that flanked the park.

Steve sat down on a vacant bench inside the playground, pulling a newspaper out of his back pocket. Then, ankle on knee, he spread the paper out on his lap and began to read. Raven watched Billy. The boy was small for his age but very agile. He went across the monkey bars at lightning speed and then proceeded to pull himself effortlessly up a rope to the top of the frame.

Then he stood, balancing precariously on the topmost bar, and waved to Steve. 'Dad, Dad, look at me!'

Steve glanced up. 'Wow, look at you! Careful now, Billy!'

He lowered his head again and Billy suddenly lurched, his arms waving about wildly as he fought to regain his balance. Raven sprang forward. Lotte grabbed him by the arm. 'What are you doing?' she gasped.

'He was about to fall . . .'

But Billy had regained his balance now and was swinging himself back down the rope. Then he ran over to the swings. 'Dad, Dad, push me!'

Steve folded his paper and got to his feet. He pulled Billy's swing back, high over his head, and then let go. Billy began to whoop and leaned far, far back on the swing, his face alight. Steve pushed him higher and higher, laughing. Billy continued to whoop into the still afternoon air.

'Maybe we should go,' Lotte said. 'It's getting cold and it'll be dark soon, and – well – we've established that Steve's got a son. There's not much more we can do today, is there?'

'Five more minutes,' Raven said. 'They won't stay much longer.'

'OK, OK,' Lotte said grumpily, hugging herself against the cold. Then she stopped, peering more closely at Raven in the dwindling light. 'What's the matter?'

'Nothing,' Raven said, turning his head away and blinking back the tears.

Minutes later, Steve and Billy were leaving the park, Billy running on ahead, his arms outstretched, making aeroplane noises. Raven and Lotte followed them back to the block of flats and then stood outside, shivering in the twilight.

'Well, maybe Billy does live with his dad,' Lotte said. 'Perhaps he and the mum have got joint custody and Billy spends one week with his dad and one week with his mum. Maybe that's why he wasn't there when we first went. I remember there was no sign of any women's things in the bathroom.' She looked at him imploringly. 'Raven, please can we go home now? I'm really tired and cold and they'll be expecting me back . . .'

Raven sighed. 'Yeah, OK. Let's go,' he said.

As they walked away, Raven glanced over his shoulder, up at the lit windows of the third floor. He thought he could just make out two figures, one tall and one small, sitting together.

On the tube Lotte rubbed her frozen hands together and bounced her knees up and down to warm herself up. Raven stared wordlessly out of the window.

'Well, at least we know now that he's got a kid,' Lotte declared over the sound of the rattling carriage. 'It looks like my theory of Steve being a two-timer is correct.'

Raven said nothing.

Lotte suddenly pushed up her coat sleeve and peered down at her watch. 'Oh no, it's already quarter to five and Mum was expecting me straight home from school today. I'd better call her and make an excuse,' she said. 'She's going to go mad.'

'What are you going to tell her?'

'I'll just say I was hanging out with a friend and lost track of time. It's the truth.' Lotte looked defensive.

Raven nodded and shrugged.

'What about you?' she asked. 'Hadn't you better ring your mum – I mean, your foster mum. Isn't she going to say anything?'

'I doubt it,' Raven said.

'That's got to be weird,' Lotte said suddenly.

'What?'

'Not – not living with your real parents. I mean, I guess it saves you a lot of hassle. They're not going to worry if you do badly at school or anything.'

'Yeah,' Raven said dully. 'It's great. I can do whatever I want. No one gives a damn.'

* * *

At the corner of the road, beside the postbox, under a tree, he stopped. The streetlamps were all lit, casting a pink glow over the quiet street. The cars sat sleeping at the kerb. This is where I live now, Raven thought. At number twelve, just five houses down. But it didn't feel like home. Bedford House hadn't felt like home either. He wondered if anywhere would feel like home again. Or perhaps he was condemned to spend the rest of his life wandering about the world, looking for a place where he felt he belonged. Did it matter now whether he walked the last fifty paces to the Russells' front door? Did it make any difference to them whether he came back or not? In all these houses, in all these streets, in all these towns and villages, were people. People behind all the brightly lit windows, going about their evening routines. If he disappeared, would any of them notice? If you didn't matter, what was the point of going on?

Chapter Seven

It was a painfully sunny Saturday morning; the winter frost had melted away and the air smelled almost like spring. At the breakfast table Ella was eating a croissant, spraying the table with crumbs as she recounted a long and involved story about her plans to sabotage the school play. Dan had just come in from a tennis match and was loud and sweaty and grinning, his hair on end.

'It's such a beautiful day,' Jackie was saying. 'Maybe we should all get out.'

'That's a good idea,' Dan agreed.

'Mummy, Mummy, Mummy, I want to go to the aquarium! No, the zoo! No, to the fair!'

'Raven, what would you like to do?' Jackie asked him.

'I've got homework—' Raven began.

Jackie drew in her breath sharply with annoyance.

'You can do your homework tomorrow,' Dan said quietly. 'Let's make the most of a sunny day.'

'How about that new adventure playground that's just opened?' Jackie suggested brightly. 'Apparently it has swinging bridges, a miniature cable car, an obstacle course, a massive twenty-metre slide—'

'Oh yes, oh yes, oh yes, I want to go there!' Ella shouted.

'Are adults allowed on it?' Dan asked.

'No, Daddy!' Ella exclaimed.

Jackie smiled at Dan. 'Shall we try it? I've got the brochure in the car.'

Dan ruffled Raven's hair. 'Come on, buddy, it will do us all good to get out.'

'Yay, yay, yay! Oh yippee, yippee, yay!' Ella cried.

She didn't stop yelling and singing and babbling for the whole of the thirty-minute drive. Raven wished she would shut up. When they got out of the car under the shadow of the towering chutes and giant climbing frames and swinging rope bridges and giant lookout towers, she was dancing at the end of Dan's arm, beside herself with excitement. Raven felt cold, shivery and tired. Screams of delight filled the air around them, the sun was too bright, the sky was too blue, everything was loud, harsh and exhausting.

They paid and went in and Ella was off like a bolt of lightning – over the bridge and onto the climbing frame, through the climbing frame and onto the swing rope, up the lookout tower and into the cable car . . . Jackie kept plucking nervously at Dan's sleeve. 'Can you see her, Dan? Where is she now? Oh my God, she's going to fall . . .'

They went into the café and sat by the window. They bought themselves coffees, and a hot chocolate for Raven. After a while Ella reappeared, bright red in the face, demanding juice. After five gulps she was off again. 'Come on, Raven,' Jackie kept saying. 'Don't you want to have a go?' or 'That slide looks terrifying, Raven!' He ignored her and sipped his hot chocolate, fixing on the clock on the café wall.

Suddenly Dan drained his cup and said, 'Right, you and me, Raven, on the obstacle course, right now.'

Raven looked at him. So did Jackie.

'I'll give you a race. Last one to the finish line is a great big sissy.'

'Oh, Dan, I don't think parents are supposed to—'

Dan ignored her. 'Do you think you can beat me? Don't you think I can fit through that tunnel or balance on that beam or climb up those ropes?'

Raven considered it and tried not to smile. The idea

of big Dan trying to crawl through the tunnel or haul himself up the ropes was faintly amusing.

Dan jumped up and zipped up his jacket. 'Come on, come on, let's go!'

Raven pulled an embarrassed face.

'I mean it,' Dan said. 'Last one to the finish line is a great big sissy!' And he dashed outside.

Jackie looked at Raven. 'Oh, Raven,' she said. 'Please go and keep an eye on him – he's going to kill himself!'

With a small smile, Raven got to his feet and followed Dan outside.

Dan was crouched at the starting line, eyeing the running, breathless children ahead of him. 'Ready?' he shouted at Raven. 'On your marks, get set, go!'

Raven broke into a run as Dan leaped over the hurdles and began swinging himself across the monkey bars, taking them two at a time. He was good and he was fast. Suddenly Raven wondered if Dan actually had any intention of letting him win. Perhaps not. He pushed himself to go faster. Through the tunnel, Dan was leading, but up the ropes Raven got level, then across the long, thin beam of wood Dan lost his balance and fell. Raven went more slowly and stayed on. Up the rope net Dan was right behind him, but suddenly he grabbed hold of Raven's leg and managed to draw level. The cheat!

Raven swung himself hard over the wooden beam and slid down the other side, the rope burning his hands, but he didn't care. He'd lost Dan, at least for the moment. Then came a series of swinging metal hoops: the drop was big, with muddy water at the bottom. Raven started off too fast and got tired in the middle; suddenly, hanging by one arm, he thought he might have to let go. He looked back and saw Dan reach for the first hoop. With a grunt, he forced himself on, reached the other side, his arms weak, jumped down, raced and touched the post at the end, and then he was running back, over the rope bridge, on the final lap. Dan had fallen at the hoops – he was going to win! And suddenly Jackie and Ella were hanging over the wooden fence at the side, shouting, 'Go on, Raven, go on, Raven!' and some other kids were watching and cheering too. As Raven threw himself at the rings, he could hear Dan behind him; over the bridge they were even but up the ropes he was much faster, and then through the tunnel and back towards the starting line and – he'd won, he'd won!

Laughing, he looked back at Dan, who arrived with a shout and collapsed in a heap on the ground, and Ella was yelling, 'Daddy, Raven beated you! Raven beated you!' and Jackie was laughing and said, 'My God, darling, are you all right?' and some other kids were laughing too. Raven gripped his knees, easing the stitch in his side, his cheeks burning, the air rasping in his throat, and Dan was picking himself up and wiping the mud from his trousers and groaning and saying to Raven, 'Christ, you're fast! I always used to beat everyone at obstacle courses!' and Jackie was patting him on the back and laughing and saying, 'Don't worry, darling, you were very good. I'm sure none of the other parents could have beaten you!'

They went back to the café and Raven drank a whole bottle of water while Dan mopped his brow and moaned about his back and Ella shouted, 'Let's go on the slide! Let's go on the slide!' and Jackie said, 'Let's have a little rest now and get some lunch, Ella, OK?' And so they had fish and chips from the stall and Dan recounted every obstacle on the course, and Raven said, 'You grabbed my leg on the rope nets, you cheat!' and Dan said, 'That wasn't cheating, that was an accident!' and Ella said, 'You cheated, Daddy! You cheated!' and Raven said, 'So who's the great big sissy?' and Dan started sucking his thumb and winding his hair round his finger until Jackie looked embarrassed and said, 'Dan, stop it!' but Ella kept on laughing and laughing and saying, 'So who's the great big sissy?' again and again.

* * *

If they had all gone home after lunch, Raven thought afterwards, everything would have been fine. In fact, it would have been more than fine. Ella wasn't whining for once, and Jackie and Dan weren't asking him endless questions and then shooting each other desperate glances over his silence, and he wasn't thinking about Steve or school, and everyone was laughing and happy. It was one of those moments that you just want to take a picture of in your mind in an attempt to preserve that point in time for ever. But of course, that didn't happen. The clock on the wall continued to tick round to four o'clock, lunch got eaten, Ella got fidgety and Jackie took her to the toilets. But when Ella came back, she was talking about the slide again. The slide. The slide.

'OK, last thing, but then we're going to go,' Dan said. 'It's starting to get dark and the park's going to shut soon.'

They put their coats back on and went towards the slide, which wasn't just an ordinary slide but a gigantic twenty-metre monster with what looked like a wall of scaffolding you had to climb up before reaching a small platform. The slide was so wide, ten people would have fitted across it, and so long, it flanked the whole of the adventure playground.

But the man at the foot of the steps took one look at Ella and said, 'She's too small.'

'She's nearly six,' Dan said. 'Can't she go on my lap?'

The man shook his head. 'Sorry,' he said. 'It's too high. Gotta be over ten.'

Ella began to wail. 'Never mind, lovey, never mind,' Jackie said. 'We'll come back when you're bigger.'

'It's not fair!' Ella cried.

'Come on,' Jackie said. 'Let's run round to the front and watch Raven and Daddy come down – shall we do that? Then we can get you some candyfloss.'

Ella sniffed. 'OK . . .'

They left. Dan looked at Raven and flashed him a grin. 'Shall we go?'

'One at a time,' the man said.

Dan shot Raven a quick roll of the eyes. 'I'll go first,' he said. 'That'll give Jackie and Ella time to get to the front of the slide and watch you come down.'

'OK,' Raven said.

Dan looked at the man, the man gave a nod and Dan began to climb the cage. Up and up he went, until he disappeared into the gathering dusk. The man looked at his stopwatch and said nothing. Raven pushed his hands into the pockets of his jacket. Suddenly he felt very cold.

The man hadn't moved. Raven looked at him. 'Can I go?' he asked.

The man shook his head. 'Gotta give him thirty seconds to clear,' he muttered.

Raven glanced back up. The lights at the top of the slide shone against a dark blue sky.

'OK, your turn,' said the man.

Raven began to climb. The metal bars felt cold and wet under his hands. He hadn't heard anything from Dan – the end of the slide was too far away. Up here the wind was stronger. Beneath him, the playground was emptying fast, the approaching dusk driving the last of the stragglers away. Now it looked almost deserted. The metal rungs continued and his legs began to ache. It was a long way up.

Then suddenly the steps ended. There was a metal platform, surrounded by steel bars. It felt like he had reached the clouds. The whole of London seemed to be spread out in the distance, winking at him in a shimmer of golden lights. Behind him, to his left and to his right, the platform was tightly encased in a framework of bars. But in front of him lay the slide, like an airport runway, flanked with red and green lights, but sloping down and out and away, the end disappearing into the darkness. It was a very long way to fall.

Gradually Raven realized that he hadn't moved for several minutes. Neither forwards, onto the slide, nor backwards, down the steps. He was suddenly, startlingly aware of not being able to move at all. The wind seemed to strengthen, making him sway. His muscles began to ache from gripping the rails and his arms began to shake. A few raindrops fell from the sky and splattered his face but he didn't dare let go to wipe them away. The wind tugged harder and he tightened his grip on the rail, holding on grimly, forcing himself to breathe. A sudden gust of wind pushed him forward, and for one awful moment his stomach left him and he thought he had begun to fall. But the cold metal was still in his hands. His fingers stayed clenched over the thin rail surrounding him, the pain in them making him aware how tightly they were gripping it, and he knew that even if he wanted to, he couldn't let go. A funny noise started in his head – a hard, jarring, clattering sort of noise: his teeth were chattering so violently that his jaw ached. He tried to stop them, tried to think. All he needed to do was kneel and climb back down; it wasn't that difficult. But it seemed as if his body had a mind of its own. His teeth continued to clatter against each other, his hands remained glued to the rail. OK, he thought, break it down. Step one, let go of the rail. Step two, put your hands down on the floor. Step three, get down on your knees. Step four, extend one foot down behind you.

Step five, place foot on top rung. But it was one thing thinking it – he could visualize it perfectly; it was another to actually do it. So he remained facing the front, still standing, his hands still clenched round the cold wet metal. Apart from the shivering, which intensified with every gust of wind, he could not move at all.

Come on, he told himself furiously. Stop being a baby. You can do it, you can do it. You're not going to fall. But his body seemed to think otherwise. Indeed his body seemed convinced that if he let go, if he moved the slightest fraction in fact, he would definitely fall. He stared down, hypnotized, at the adventure playground below. What would it be like to fall all that way? Would you scream? Would you have time to shut your eyes before you hit the ground? And when you landed, you would look like a crumpled thing – not real, kind of like a rag doll in clothes – and one of your shoes would have fallen off and you wouldn't move at all. There wouldn't be much blood, only a thin trickle from the corner of your mouth. People would rush over to you, bend over you, and someone would pull out a mobile phone and call an ambulance. By the time the ambulance arrived, a small gaggle of bystanders would have formed and one of them would be looking up, pointing at the third-floor balcony. When the ambulance arrived, the green paramedics would put a fat white collar round your neck, press your chest and blow in your mouth. But after a while they would stop, look at their watches, write something down, lift you onto a stretcher, replace your missing shoe, smooth down your skirt, then cover you with a white sheet and lift you into the ambulance. And you would never see her again.

He had begun to tremble so much, he was afraid his hands might slip off the rail. His eyes watered till the lights from below grew blurred and jumpy. His back and neck started to ache so much, he was forced to rest his forehead against his hand. He couldn't believe how much it hurt, just standing here, doing nothing. He desperately needed to pee.

Hours seemed to pass. He felt as if he had been stuck there for ever. The memory of the obstacle course seemed like a lifetime away. He could not believe there had been any *before* or would be any *after*. It seemed as if his whole life had been this cold rail, this hard ledge and this huge drop of twenty metres or more onto the concrete below. Then he heard a sound, a voice, behind him. 'Raven, are you there? Raven, what on earth are you doing? We've been waiting for you for ages! What's going on?'

He couldn't reply, couldn't shout. He tried to draw

breath but no sound came out. Suddenly there was movement behind him and Dan's hand appeared on his shoulder. 'Raven, what's the matter? What are you staring at?' Dan covered Raven's hands with his own. Raven's fingers seemed to have frozen and Dan tried to uncurl them and pull them off the rail. 'Hey, buddy, it's OK. I've got you. You're perfectly safe. We're just going to kneel and go back down the steps. All you have to do is let go and kneel down. I've got you, I've got you.'

Suddenly there was nothing holding him. A strangled sob escaped him.

'I've got you, I've got you. Look, I'm right here, you can't possibly fall. I'm right behind you.' Dan put an arm round his waist and gripped him tight and told him what to do with his hands and feet, and they began to climb down together.

It took for ever. Raven's fingers were so cold he could hardly feel them. Moving each foot down a rung seemed to take all the strength he had. 'Don't let go,' he said, his teeth chattering loudly in his mouth. 'Don't let go, don't let go, don't let go.'

'I'm not going to let go, Raven,' Dan said. 'I promise. Matey, I'll never let you fall.'

They finally reached the ground. Raven was so wobbly he could hardly stand. He felt Dan envelop him in a tight, strong hug. 'You're all right, mate,' Dan whispered. 'You're all right.' Raven clung to him. He never wanted Dan to let go.

Jackie and Ella were standing back, silent, their eyes wide. Dan gripped him by the shoulders and walked him back to the car park. In the car Dan turned on the heat and Jackie said softly, 'Oh, Dan, we should have thought, we should have thought . . .'

Raven couldn't stop shivering. Ella reached out her hand and touched his. 'It's all right, Raven,' she said. 'I would've caught you if you'd falled.'

The next day was Sunday. Raven sat at his desk in front of the large bay window and tried to get a handle on his maths homework. But it was difficult to concentrate. There were so many things he didn't want to think about, and yet, like an overheated room full of trapped people, they kept clamouring to be let out. Music thumped from downstairs – Ella was doing her dance routine for the fifth time that morning. Now it sounded like she was singing too. She had been up early, making tickets to give out to the neighbours for her forthcoming concert – which by the sounds of things she was now rehearsing. She was actually planning to charge the neighbours five pounds each to come and watch her sing and dance. Raven wondered how Dan and Jackie were going to get out of that one. It astonished him that *anyone* could be so shockingly self-confident, let alone a five-year-old.

Then there came a knock on the door. Raven turned round. Dan came in. 'Need a hand?'

Raven shook his head.

Dan came in anyway, closed the door against the beat of Superstar, and sat down on the end of the bed. 'What are you doing?' he asked lightly.

'Homework,' Raven said.

Dan laughed. 'I can see that! What subject?'

'Maths,' Raven said. 'Algebra.'

Dan picked up Lotte's crumpled page from the Internet. 'What's this? Oh, that's a nice picture of Billy!'

Raven swung himself round in the swivel chair to face Dan and eyed him warily. He had a feeling that Dan had come to see him to speak about something else and was beating about the bush.

Dan looked at him steadily. 'You must have given yourself quite a fright yesterday,' he began.

Raven leaned back in his chair and narrowed his eyes, swivelling himself gently one way and then the other with his big toe.

'You gave *us* quite a fright.' Dan smiled briefly. 'You

know there's a doctor,' he went on, 'who can help with things like that.'

Raven looked at him. 'I'm not going to see another bloody psychiatrist,' he said.

'I know you're sick of that,' Dan said, 'but maybe we can find someone—'

'My mum's dead,' Raven said flatly. 'Nothing anyone says or does is going to bring her back. I know that. I'm fine. I'm sorry about yesterday.'

Dan stared at him and then made a gesture of helplessness. 'Raven, I can't imagine what it's like for you. Losing your mother at such a young age and in such a terrible way, it's an awful, awful thing. But terrible accidents do happen. And everyone gets angry sometimes. You mustn't ever blame yourself. But there are people – people that can help . . .'

Raven met Dan's imploring gaze. 'No there aren't,' he said.

'I remember how I felt when my father died,' Dan said quietly. 'I didn't want to talk about it with anyone. I blamed myself terribly. Even though everyone said it wasn't my fault, I felt as if somehow my bad behaviour had precipitated his heart attack . . .'

Raven allowed himself to look at Dan. 'But it wasn't your fault, was it?'

Dan's eyes were fierce. 'Of course not.'

Raven stared at Dan. His expression was earnest, as if he honestly believed what he had just said. Raven felt a sharp pain start up behind his eyes. He looked away quickly. 'I'd better get on with my homework,' he managed.

Dan came over and put his arm round Raven's shoulders and gave him a tight squeeze. For a brief moment Raven felt as if he was going to lose it, as if the tears crowding behind his eyes were about to overwhelm him completely. He bit his tongue hard and tensed his muscles and waited for Dan to withdraw his arm again. 'I just think it would be helpful for you to see someone, a specialist who helps traumatized young people. Just consider it. Will you at least think about it?' Dan said softly.

Raven mumbled a non-committal reply and turned back to his desk, back to the rows of neat equations that blurred and fragmented on the page.

Chapter Eight

Raven put down his pen and raised his gaze to survey the sea of lowered heads around him. Over twenty different shades of brown, a couple of dirty blonds, one redhead, ponytails, plaits, fuzz, spikes, two shaved heads, a mohican . . . The backs of twenty-eight white shirts, twenty-eight hands holding twenty-eight pens, biros scratching across paper as Mr Miles's voice droned on. But he, number twenty-nine, had stopped writing. Had lifted his eyes from the page in front of him, already half filled with untidy scrawl, to prop his chin on his hand and stare around. To stare out over all those heads, all those thoughts, all those different personalities. With those heads he only shared pictures of school – of the classrooms, of the teachers, of the playground. Those heads were completely shut off from his – he didn't know what they thought about, what they liked or disliked, or what had been the worst thing to have ever happened to them. For all he knew, those heads were empty, just robots posing as humans. Except for the blond mohican of Kyle and the brown fuzz of Brett behind him. Those heads, he knew, were real. Those heads got a kick out of laughing at him, out of seeing him hurt or humiliated. And those heads reminded him that he was real, too. That he hadn't turned into a robot after Mum died, that his emotions hadn't evaporated with her, that his eyes could still ache with suppressed tears, that he could still feel lonely and frightened.

But the blonde ponytail with the red elastic belonged to Lotte, and her head contained some of the same pictures as his – Steve's balding head, for instance, or the street where he lived. It made him feel strange, but somehow reassured, to know that she shared some of his secrets. Just staring at the back of her head made the whole day feel a little less unbearable. He had never imagined he could be mates with a girl before. He had never imagined he could actually like *anyone* in this shitty school.

Halfway through the history test there was a sharp whack on the back of his head and something fell to the floor beside his chair. Swinging round in his seat,

Raven glared at the bent heads behind him. Several pupils glanced up at him in surprise, but in the back row Kyle and Brett kept their heads down, still writing. He turned back to his desk and almost instantly there was another sharp whack, this time catching the back of his ear. Raven's chair scraped against the floor with an angry screech as he swung himself back round.

'Sit still, will you?' Mr Miles snapped. 'Raven, if you can't keep your eyes on your own page then I'm going to fail you on this test.'

Realizing that any attempts to protest his innocence would just amuse his persecutors further, Raven forced himself to turn back to the front and ignore the murmurs from behind. From her place by the window Lotte shot him a sympathetic look. Raven picked up his pen, his hand shaking with anger. Then there was another whack. This time it hurt. And a small stone landed on the desk in front of him. He turned in time to see Kyle and Brett snorting with laughter.

Raven raised the binoculars to his eyes and peered through them up at Steve's flat. He was definitely in: one window was lit, even though it wasn't quite dark yet. Suddenly he heard footsteps and dropped the binoculars round his neck, stepping quickly behind a tree. 'I knew I'd find you here!' a voice exclaimed loudly.

It was Lotte. 'Shh!' Raven frowned at her in annoyance. 'What are you doing?' She was conspicuous and noisy with her bright pink jacket and windswept hair.

'You weren't at the bus stop, and then I saw you going into the tube station, so I figured you were coming here,' Lotte replied. 'Why didn't you tell me you were going to Steve's?'

'Because I'm not doing anything yet, I'm just – I'm just gathering evidence,' Raven replied quickly.

'You've got binoculars,' Lotte noted. 'Good idea!'

'They're Dan's. I nicked them from home. They're really powerful – take a look,' he said, removing the strap from his neck and handing them to her.

She raised them to her eyes, fiddling with the focus wheel. 'But we're at too much of an angle,' she complained. 'And now the sun's bouncing off the window—'

Raven quickly yanked her arm down. 'Stop! There's a woman staring at us.'

Lotte quickly put the binoculars behind her back. 'Oh, shit, is she going to come over?'

They waited anxiously, scuffling their shoes against the pavement and looking down at the ground. After what seemed like an age, the woman and her dog moved on.

'We can't stand and use the binoculars here,' Lotte

declared when the woman had gone. 'The neighbours are going to get suspicious. They might even call the police.'

Raven stepped back and looked up at the tall houses behind them. There were no signs of peeping grannies at the windows but you could never be sure . . . His eyes lit on the boarded-up house directly opposite Steve's flat. Suddenly he had an idea.

'If we could find a way of getting into that empty house . . .'

Lotte turned to stare at him. 'You gotta be kidding me.'

'One of the boards is bound to be loose. If we get off the street and try a window at the back of the house, nobody would ever see—'

'Oh my God, that's breaking and entering!'

'It's a *derelict* house!'

'It still might belong to somebody!'

'Hardly! It's probably just been repossessed or belongs to the council.'

Lotte looked at him, wide-eyed and afraid.

'Look, if we stay here staring any longer, people are definitely going to get suspicious,' Raven said. 'Let's try and get into the garden at least and see if there are any loose boards at the back of the house.'

The boarded-up house was semi-detached, separated

from its neighbour by a narrow door leading between the houses to the garden. Empty bins stood in front of it and grass sprouted up from underneath. Clearly it had not been opened for a very long time. Raven pushed on it, expecting to find it locked, but the wood was rotting and he almost fell through. He motioned to Lotte. 'Quick!'

Glancing nervously up and down the street, she turned and hurried after him. The garden they found themselves in was tiny and overgrown. Knee-high grass and trailing ivy greeted them. Lotte hit her leg on something and gasped. A rusty part of an old motorbike. Behind the house, away from the streetlamps, it was very dark. Lotte clutched the back of Raven's arm as he began to feel his way around the first boarded-up window. It didn't give. He moved to the other side of the back door and began feeling the boarding of the other window. It too was firmly nailed against the frame. However, if he tugged as hard as he could at the bottom right-hand corner, a slight rattling sound could be heard. He picked up a short thick stick from beneath the tree.

'You can't break it down!' Lotte exclaimed. 'Somebody will—'

'I'm going to prise it open, silly!'

She bit her lower lip and watched him silently, the whites of her eyes visible in the darkness.

Raven dumped his school bag in the long grass and got to work, one foot braced against the wall, pulling the corner of the board towards him with all his strength. At first nothing seemed to happen, then after several minutes of huffing and puffing there was a sharp crack and he stumbled backwards. Lotte gasped and threw herself down in the grass as a dog started barking.

Raven froze, crouched down by the wall, waiting for the sound of raised voices and spotlights, but none came. The dog stopped barking. He straightened up and examined the boarding. A piece had broken off the bottom right corner. He reached inside. Cold damp air. 'If we leave our bags here, I reckon we could just about squeeze through.'

Lotte put her hands over her mouth, her breathing audible. 'C-can't we come back when it's light?'

'No, we're less likely to be spotted when it's dark.'

'Shouldn't we – couldn't we come back with a torch or something?'

'We'd be seen!'

Lotte said nothing. Her teeth were chattering even though the evening was mild.

'You could wait for me here if you want,' Raven suggested.

'No, I'll – I'll come.'

'It'll be all right. There'll only be dust and spiders.'

'OK.' She didn't sound too thrilled.

'I'll go first,' Raven said. He took his blazer off and tossed it on top of his bag. Then he hoisted one leg over the windowsill and started to squeeze himself through on his stomach. The splintered ends of the board scraped against his back and the windowsill dug painfully into his ribcage. He landed on soft, damp floorboards. It was very dark. He stood up and peered back through the gap. 'Come on, it's fine.'

Lotte poked her leg in tentatively. Then her arm. He gave it a pull to help her and there was a loud tearing noise before she tumbled to the floor.

'Oh, shit,' Lotte said, examining the ripped shoulder of her school shirt. 'Mum's going to be furious.'

They stood facing each other, one hand on the window frame, reluctant to leave the only small source of light. 'We've got to try and find the stairs and get to the top of the house,' Raven said.

'But it's pitch black!'

'It's not. Our eyes just aren't used to the darkness. Anyway, we can feel our way.'

'How?'

'Hold onto my shoulder,' Raven said, stretching his

arms out into the cold, musty blackness and taking a few tentative steps. The floorboards creaked and he could feel something crunchy underfoot. Starting from the window with the broken board, he began feeling his way along the wall. Lotte's fingers dug into his shoulder.

The blackness was like a mask, suffocating, oppressing. There seemed to be no depth to it: he felt as if there was a great wall right in front of his eyes and any minute he might crash into it. After a minute or so the back of his neck began to ache from keeping his head pulled back. When his hands reached a gap in the wall, an empty door frame, it was an effort of will to force his feet to walk through it. It was like his mind was telling him to do one thing and his body was telling him to do another. Logically he knew that the worst thing he was likely to stumble across was a load of spiders, but his body felt as if he were walking into a lion's den. At one point a loose floorboard made him stumble and he had to bite his tongue to stop himself from crying out, his mind picturing a bottomless hole. At last he found some stairs and cautiously began to climb, testing each step for rotting wood before allowing his whole weight onto it. Lotte's grip on his shoulder was vice-like and her chattering teeth were right behind his ear. They reached the first-floor landing without incident. Then Lotte whispered, 'What if someone sees the hole and comes and boards it up while we're still inside?'

'It's evening, silly. There won't be any builders around at this time.'

'But what if someone like a neighbour notices?'

'They won't,' Raven said with more conviction than he felt. He found himself recalling a nightmare he used to have that he was swimming underwater and somebody had covered the pool with a sheet of glass. He was beginning to feel cold now and it was an effort to keep from shivering – he didn't want Lotte to feel it. Suddenly Lotte tightened her grip painfully. 'Shh!'

They froze. There was a sound from outside. Voices?

Oh Jesus, Raven thought. We've been spotted. We're dead.

The voices faded. The only sound was the desperate thumping of his heart. They continued upwards and spotted a faint glow seeping down from the top of the stairwell.

'Nearly there – the top windows aren't boarded up, remember?'

They hurried up the last flight of stairs, and opened the door into a large loft lit by the streetlamps, with bare floorboards and sloping ceilings, a couple of large empty crates and two tall windows looking out over the street.

'Thank goodness!' Lotte exclaimed, running over to them. Then she gave a loud gasp.

'What?' he barked at her.

'Look!'

Across the road, in a brightly lit curtainless window, a figure sat at a table. Raven quickly lifted the binoculars from around his neck. A kitchen table, and then Steve's unshaven face leaped into focus. Raven took a step back and let go of the binoculars. It was like being in the same room.

'What's he doing?' Lotte asked.

They knelt on the floorboards, elbows on the windowsill. Raven lifted the binoculars to his eyes again.

'Eating, it looks like,' he said. Steve had a newspaper laid out on the table beside his plate and his feet up on a chair. The flickering light from the corner of the room suggested the television was also on. Suddenly a cropped brown head bobbed up above the side of the table. 'Billy's there too.'

'What's he doing?' Lotte asked again.

'Dunno – oh, he's climbing up on a chair; he's about to have dinner.' Raven watched as Steve leaned over and started cutting up the food on Billy's plate. Billy propped his head up on his hand and smiled.

'Bastard,' Raven said.

Lotte started. 'What?'

He lowered the binoculars. 'Just sitting there, all cosy and innocent.' His throat ached. 'Wait here, I've got an idea.'

'What? Where are you going?'

He hurried back down the stairs, back into the damp darkness. He whacked his knee against the door frame in his hurry to get back outside. For a moment he was disorientated, with no idea which way to turn. Then he spotted the broken board, the gap casting a faint glow. In the garden his hands scrabbled around in the grass until he found what he was looking for.

Back upstairs, Lotte was upset. 'Why d'you go charging off like that? I didn't know where you were! I thought maybe you weren't— What are you doing?'

He was struggling with the windows, unscrewing the rusty lock, pulling up the sash.

'Somebody will see!' Lotte gasped.

'No they won't.' The bottom half of the window slid up with an angry squeak.

'What have you got in your hands?'

Raven took a big step away from the window and drew back his arm.

'Raven, don't!' Lotte shrieked.

The first stone missed its target. Bounced off the

windowsill and, with a dull thud, fell into the street below. The second was a better shot. It hit Steve's kitchen window with a crack. Raven stepped closer to the open window and put all his effort into the third. The sound of breaking glass startled him. There was a shout. Lotte grabbed his arm and pulled him to the floor.

They crouched on their hands and knees, the dust from the floorboards tickling the backs of their throats, their rapid breathing rasping through the silence. Then came a man's voice from the street below. 'Who the hell was that?'

Raven's muscles twitched with the desire to jump up again but Lotte's fingers dug into his arm. The shout came again: 'Who the hell threw that stone?'

Raven was sure that their breathing must be audible to whoever was in the street below. All he had to do was glance up and spot the open window. They would be trapped. Several moments of silence followed. Raven wondered whether Steve had gone back inside. He uncurled Lotte's fingers from around his wrist and crawled over to the window. Slowly, carefully, he raised his head to peep over the sill.

Steve was standing there, in the middle of the road, hands on his hips, looking up and down the street. The door of his block was ajar and in the light stood a little boy in pyjamas. Raven fingered his last stone. Steve turned away. 'Come on, Billy, let's go back upstairs. It's probably just some bored kids with nothing better to do.' He started back up the steps to the door. Raven drew back his arm and let fly.

There was a yell and Steve's hand went to his head. He leaped up the remaining steps, grabbing Billy by the arm, and rushed inside, slamming the door behind him.

Lotte was up on her knees, staring at Raven, her mouth open. 'Did you hit him?'

Raven looked at her. 'No. Just scared him.'

'Shit!' Lotte gave a half-laugh, her eyes still wide. 'You're crazy. I can't believe you just did that.'

'It was only to scare him,' Raven said.

'Well, I guess he deserves that much.' She didn't sound too convinced.

'We should get out of here,' Raven said.

Lotte got up and approached the open window. 'What's he doing now?'

'No, we *really* should get out of here,' Raven said. He knew what Steve would be doing now.

'He's back upstairs, speaking on the phone—' Lotte whispered. 'Oh no, d'you think he's calling the police?'

Raven pulled the sash down and grabbed her hand. 'Come on, we've got to hurry.'

It was a scramble to make their way back to the

broken board. In his haste, Raven misjudged the stairs and fell down the last three steps. He felt his foot twist beneath him as he landed and a jolt of pain made him gasp.

'Shit, are you all right?'

He bit the side of his hand to stop himself from crying out and crouched motionless in the darkness, weak with pain.

'Are you hurt?' Lotte asked.

He breathed deeply, fighting to stay calm. Pain shot through his ankle with terrifying intensity. He didn't want to move. Pulling himself up on the banister, he felt the sweat break out over the back of his neck.

'Raven, say something!'

He put his foot down on the ground and almost passed out. 'OK,' he managed breathlessly, 'I may have sprained my ankle . . .'

'Oh no, oh no,' Lotte gasped. 'Can you walk? Shall I help you?'

'It's all right,' he managed breathlessly. 'Can you see the broken board?'

'I'll check,' Lotte said. Suddenly she screamed.

'What?' he shouted.

'Spider web! Yuk!' Lotte said.

'Try and hurry—'

'OK, OK . . . I see a light . . . Here, over here!'

Raven leaned on Lotte's shoulder and followed her, hobbling. The light momentarily disappeared as she began to squeeze herself out of the opening. When it was Raven's turn, he put his hurt leg through first. But this meant that when he reached the other side, his twisted ankle had to take the full weight of his body. He rolled onto the grass and had to bite his tongue to keep from crying out.

'Get up, get up!' Lotte was whispering urgently. 'Oh help, help!'

There were voices. Close by. The other side of the garden door, coming from the street.

'. . . it was definitely a stone,' one voice was saying. 'Billy picked it up off the kitchen floor. But the one that hit me seemed to come from above, from one of the trees maybe . . .'

'Those vandals could have climbed up a tree,' came a second voice, also male.

Lotte grabbed hold of Raven's hand and crushed it.

'P'raps we should wait for the police to get here – no need to make ourselves an unnecessary target—'

'Hold on, let's just have a look back here . . .' The voices were approaching the rotting fence door that separated the garden from the street. Raven pulled Lotte towards him so that his mouth touched her ear. 'If they open the door and come into the garden, you've got to make a run for it. Go over that wall there. You'll have to climb through a couple of gardens but then you should hit the next street. There's no point in us both getting caught.'

Lotte seemed to be holding her breath, her eyes huge in the darkness.

'It couldn't be from there – that house is boarded up,' came the second voice.

'Oh well, the cops should be here soon,' said Steve.

The voices retreated. Lotte let out her breath in a rush. Raven fought to stay calm. 'Listen,' he whispered carefully. 'We can't go out the way we came. For all we know, Steve and his mate are standing at the door waiting for the cops to arrive.'

'Let's go back into the house then!'

'No. The police might decide to search it. We have to go through the gardens to reach the next street.'

'But how—?' Lotte began.

'If I hold onto your shoulder, I can limp,' Raven said. 'I'll need to get you to give me a leg-up over the walls, that's all. As long as there aren't any dogs waiting for us, we should be OK.'

Lotte let out a whimper. 'Why can't we just wait here?'

'We'll be caught,' Raven said matter-of-factly.

She took a deep breath to steady herself. 'OK. What d'you want me to do?'

'First, push back that piece of boarding, we don't want to give away our watchtower,' Raven said. 'Good, now pick up our bags and blazers and just start walking, slowly.'

Lotte did as she was told. Raven found that limping was possible, so long as he remembered to put as much weight as possible on Lotte's shoulder. They reached the garden wall and Lotte threw the bags over and gave him a boost up. Using his good leg, he scrabbled for a foot hold. When he reached the top, he let himself slide down the other side. Lotte joined him with a gasp. Then they were shuffling over the flagstones to the next wall. This one was harder to climb. It took Raven four tries before he managed to reach the top with Lotte's help. Then, when he landed on one leg on the other side, a security light came on, blinding them. 'Keep going,' he said to Lotte between gritted teeth. 'Just ignore it.'

It was a frantic scramble over the next wall, fuelled by desperation to get away from the light that flooded the neatly mown lawn. But it was the last garden and Raven's good leg buckled beneath him as he landed on the pavement. Lotte jumped down beside him and they stood still for a moment under the gentle glow of a streetlamp, just trying to get their breath. Raven felt sick with exhaustion. His good leg ached like crazy and his bad ankle throbbed with pain.

'We made it!' Lotte gasped. But as she spoke, the distant wail of a siren broke the still evening air.

'Oh shit,' Raven breathed.

'That man wasn't joking when he said he'd called the cops!' Lotte said frantically.

'Let's get out of here. Come on,' Raven said.

They shuffled their way back to the tube station. By this time it was almost deserted and the ticket inspector gave Raven a strange look as he hobbled his way down to the platform. Only when they were on the tube did he allow himself to relax and then found he could barely sit up. Lotte was silent too, her face white with exhaustion.

Chapter Nine

It was cold in the boarded-up house. Beneath him, the streetlamps lit the trees with an orange glow. Occasionally a car would swish by almost soundlessly and disappear into the night. Raven's knees hurt from kneeling on the damp floorboards and his ankle still ached. He had told Dan and Jackie that he had twisted it in a game of football and they had believed him. They weren't to know that no one at school ever asked him to join in their games. He had been here for nearly half an hour now, watching through the window, but nothing had happened. There was a light on in the corridor of Steve's flat, but the kitchen and the bedrooms next door were dark. He knew where they both were. In the living room, on the other side of the flat. The television would be on and Steve would be watching it, his feet up on the coffee table amidst piles of newspapers, overflowing ashtrays, the odd Coke can . . . Billy would be having his dinner on the carpet, playing with puzzles or Lego. Steve would be dozing in his armchair, forgetting Billy's bed time . . . But suddenly the light in a bedroom went on. Billy walked in, munching something and kicking off his grey school trousers. Then he pulled his jumper over his head and struggled for a moment as it got stuck round his ears. He climbed into bed, still in his T-shirt and pants. No carefully ironed pyjamas any more. Steve came in, walked over to the window and drew the curtains. They only went halfway across. Billy was tunnelling under the duvet. Steve was sitting on the edge of the bed, picking up a book off the floor. Billy had now emerged from beneath his duvet and was snuggling up to his father. Steve settled back on the pillows beside him and began to read. Raven could see their two faces, lit by the glow of the bedside lamp. They would be reading the book together, one page each. Billy would be good at doing the different voices.

Later that night Ella stood silhouetted in the doorway, her finger in her mouth. 'What's the matter, Raven?'

'Go back to bed!' He rubbed the back of his hand over his face and rolled over to face the wall.

'I can't sleep,' Ella said. 'I got up for a wee and then I heard you crying. Why are you crying?'

'I'm not!' But he was. He put his hands over his face and tried to hold his breath but a sob escaped him.

Ella climbed up onto the bed and stroked his arm. 'Poor Raven,' she whispered. 'Don't cry, Raven, don't cry. Are you sad about your mummy?'

'Go away.'

'You can share my mummy with me.'

'Leave me alone.'

'I'm glad your mummy died,' Ella said suddenly.

Raven took his hands away from his face in astonishment. 'What?'

'Because it meant that you came to live with us.'

'So?' It was an effort not to shout at her.

'So I'm not an only child any more. I don't like being an only child.'

'You're still an only child,' Raven said. 'I'm not your brother, for Christ's sake.'

'Yes you are. You're my foster brother, and that's nearly the same thing,' Ella said. 'I always wanted a brother. Not a sister because she would steal my toys. But I like having a big brother.'

Raven stared at her in disbelief, the tears drying on his cheeks. 'I'm not *staying* here.'

'Yes you are! I'm going to tell Mummy and Daddy to keep you!' Ella shouted, wrapping her arms round his waist and pressing her head against his chest.

Raven didn't move from where he sat, propped up against his pillows, with Ella clinging to him like a limpet. Then, slowly, carefully, he leaned down and rested his chin on the top of her head. Her hair smelled of lemon shampoo.

In history the following afternoon, Mr Miles said he had a headache and told the class to summarize a long and uninteresting passage about the Stuarts from their text-books. Then he sat down at his desk and began doing some marking. A gentle hum of restlessness gradually began to rise from the class. Some people were copying the passage, others were doing their maths homework, others still were drawing. Somebody made a farting noise with their mouth and a group of kids tittered.

'Quiet!' Mr Miles snapped without looking up.

Lotte looked as if she was doing her algebra home-work. Brett was tearing off pieces of paper and rolling them into pellets and flicking them at the back of Benny's neck. Kyle had his head lowered and actually seemed to be writing . . . Raven opened his history book and gazed down at the print.

'Be quiet, will you!' Mr Miles snapped as snorts of laughter began again from another part of the class. The two boys sitting behind Kyle and Brett had stood up and were leaning over their desks, trying to see what Kyle was writing. Brett was pressing his fist to his mouth, head down, shoulders shaking. Then Kyle raised his head, folded the piece of paper he'd been writing on in half and passed it to Brett. Brett took it, unfolded it and snorted loudly with laughter, earning another irritated 'Shh' from the teacher. Brett's neighbour was leaning across the aisle now, trying to see what was going on as Brett picked up his pen, jotted something down, then carefully refolded the piece of paper and passed it on. No doubt they were drawing rude pictures again, or writing dirty jokes, or sketching a caricature of Mr Miles . . . Raven lowered his chin to rest on his folded arms. God, he was bored . . .

Suddenly he was aware of being looked at. He glanced up and saw with a start that six or seven kids from Kyle and Brett's row had turned round in their seats and were looking at him, grinning or biting their lips in an effort not to laugh. The piece of paper had reached Benny in the third row, and after opening it, he too snorted and turned round to look at Raven. Raven bit the side of his thumb, feeling the heat rising in his cheeks. What had

Kyle written about him? What note was it that was now
doing the rounds? Benny gave a nervous snort and
passed the note quickly to his neighbour. And the whole
charade was repeated. Raven looked desperately at Mr
Miles. Didn't the stupid teacher notice something was
going on? Why didn't he look up from his marking and
confiscate the damn note?

The note was progressing rapidly now, across the
third row and back to the fourth. Kids from the row
behind were craning their necks now to try and see, and
Raven realized with a sudden lurch that the note was
now approaching Lotte, who hadn't yet looked up from
her maths book. There were more sniggers, another
'Silence!' from Mr Miles, and then Lotte's neighbour was
reaching across the aisle and tapping her on the
shoulder. First she shrugged him off, then, when
the tapping was repeated, she put down her pen and
looked across with an irritated sigh. The boy held out the
note. She gave him a condescending look and took it
from him. Raven felt his muscles twitch and fought the
urge to jump up and snatch it out of her hand. At least
Lotte would put a stop to it, wouldn't she? *Wouldn't
she?* Lotte unfolded the piece of paper. She didn't move
for a moment. Then she too turned to look at Raven,
but with something like pity in her eyes. She started

mouthing something to him, but then the bell rang and Carla, sitting behind her, reached over and grabbed the paper from her hand.

'Homework – first ten questions on Chapter Four!' Mr Miles yelled above the din before heading out of the classroom.

Raven pushed his way over to Carla. She opened the note, started to laugh and then, seeing him coming, passed it quickly to her neighbour.

'Hey!' Kyle shouted, going to the front of the class and waving his arms in the air to get everyone's attention. 'Don't go home before you've seen our special photo! Who hasn't seen it yet? Sarah and Sophie?'

The twins shook their heads nervously and hurried away. 'Georgia? Angie?'

Raven lunged at Harriet, who was now holding the piece of paper and pulling a horrified face, and tore it from her hand. He just had time to see a photo of a naked woman, cut out of a porn magazine, with the scrawled words underneath: *Doesn't Raven look just like his mum?* He froze in shock. With a whoop, Kyle snatched the magazine page out of Raven's hand. 'Hey, you two, look here, have you seen this?'

Two girls in the doorway stopped, looked at the paper in Kyle's hand and pulled a face. 'That's disgusting!' one said. Other kids crowded round Kyle. 'What's disgusting? Let's see!'

An explosion went off inside Raven's head and he launched himself into the huddle. Several of the others jumped out of the way as he grabbed Kyle by the collar of his shirt and dragged him to the floor. Kyle yelled and lashed out with his feet but Raven tore the paper from his hand and started kicking him in the ribs.

Kyle pulled Raven down on top of him and suddenly there were chairs and desks and shouts and kicks and people crowding all around . . . Then somebody had him by the hair in a vice-like grip and was pulling him away, lifting him almost off the ground and slamming him against the wall. 'You little fuck. D'you really wanna fight?' It was Brett, his face red with anger, his hand around Raven's throat, cutting off his air supply.

With all the strength he could muster, Raven kneed him in the groin. Brett let go and staggered backwards, gasping, his face registering complete astonishment.

Kyle had got to his feet and was readying himself for another attack. He lunged forward, his fist raised, just as Raven grabbed for the nearest chair, holding it out in front of him and forcing Kyle back.

'Oh, come *on*,' Kyle sneered breathlessly. 'You really think you can suddenly turn all tough? Everyone knows you're just a cry baby and your dead mum was a fucking whore!' He took a tentative step forward and reached out to grab one of the legs of the chair.

Raven slammed the chair legs into Kyle's body with brute force. Kyle went shooting backwards, crashing into several desks and then collapsing on the floor. He didn't get up. He didn't even move. Brett stood frozen against the classroom wall. Raven jumped over Kyle's inert figure, grabbed his bag and blazer, pushed past the gaggle of stunned onlookers and ran from the room.

'I knew I'd find you here.' Lotte stood in the doorway at the top floor of the empty house, her face still in the shadows, her scuffed black shoes and white ankle socks lit eerily by the torch that lay on the floor. 'Are you OK?'

Raven didn't reply.

'You should have seen the look on Kyle and Brett's faces when you went for them. They were scared shitless.'

'Is Kyle dead?' Raven asked dully.

'No!' Lotte looked shocked at the idea. 'Of course not. He was just moaning and groaning a lot when the nurse arrived, saying that all his bones had been broken and he couldn't possibly move.'

Raven felt himself relax slightly and the shivering that had gripped him ever since he'd run from the classroom began to fade. 'Oh well, that's it then. I'll probably be expelled again and Dan and Jackie will send me back to the unit.' He felt numb, as if nothing could really hurt him any more.

'You won't be expelled. All the teachers know that Kyle and Brett are bullies. And everyone who saw the fight will say that Kyle and Brett started it. They're all delighted that someone's finally had the guts to stand up to those two.'

Silence descended. Raven stared at the opposite wall. Lotte came to sit on one of the crates and looked at him, leaning against the wall, his legs stretched out in front of him, his penknife in his hand.

'You were expelled from your last school then?'

Raven just nodded.

'How come?'

His eyes did not meet hers. 'Stopped talking.'

'What d'you mean?'

'I mean that I stopped talking.'

'You stopped talking completely?'

'Yes.'

'For how long?'

'Couple of months.'

'Fuck.' Lotte sounded impressed. Her eyes suddenly locked onto the penknife. 'What are you doing with that?'

'Nothing.'

Her eyes narrowed. 'Is that blood on your shirt?'

Raven flicked the penknife closed and put it back in his pocket. Lotte got up and knelt down on the floor-boards beside him. Before he had time to move away, she grabbed his arm and pushed up his blood-flecked sleeve, staring down at the bloody array of cuts across the inside of his arm.

'Fucking hell!'

Raven pulled his arm away angrily.

Lotte sat back on her heels, her eyes wide. 'Jesus,' she breathed.

Raven angrily yanked down his sleeve.

'You did that?' Her voice was faint.

He closed his eyes and let his head fall back against the wall.

'You *did* that to yourself?' she asked softly. 'Why?'

Raven didn't answer.

'Doesn't it hurt?'

'Course.'

'So why d'you do it?'

He shrugged again. 'It helps,' he said.

'Helps what?'

'Helps me feel better.'

'But how?' Lotte asked. 'How can hurting yourself

make you feel better? If I hurt myself, I feel worse. If I hurt myself badly, I just want to cry.'

'It's the opposite. It takes away the pain.'

'What pain?'

'The pain inside my head.'

'Like a headache, you mean?'

'No. Inside my mind.'

Lotte said nothing for a moment. 'You mean because of Kyle and Brett? Because you're living in a foster home?' She gazed at him steadily, then added softly, 'Because of your mum? Because of how much you hate Steve?'

Raven's eyes met hers. 'No,' he said, 'because of how much I hate me.'

Lotte was silent. She moved over to sit beside him against the wall. Their arms were almost touching, but not quite. Side by side, they stared straight ahead into the darkness.

'You shouldn't,' Lotte said. 'You shouldn't hate yourself. You're the best friend I ever had. Before you came along I had no one to talk to. And my so-called friends all bored me to death.'

A long pause. 'You wouldn't want to be friends with me,' Raven said. 'Not if you really knew me.'

'I do know you. And it's not just me. Ella's crazy about

you. And I bet Jackie and Dan really care about you too.'

Raven got up suddenly and walked over to the window. 'None of you know me,' he said, his voice harsh. 'None of you. You don't know me at all.'

Lotte said nothing. 'Sometimes I feel like that too,' she began. 'But it's just because you're feeling kinda fed up—'

Raven turned abruptly from the window. 'I should have killed Kyle,' he said.

Lotte shuddered suddenly and pulled her knees up under her school coat. 'You shouldn't say things like that. I know he's a complete twat, but—'

'You don't think I mean it?' He looked at her steadily. 'You don't think I'm capable of killing someone?'

She hesitated for a moment. 'I'm sure you *feel* like killing both of them,' she began. 'But it's not the same as actually—'

'Everyone's capable of murder.' Raven cut her off, his voice hard, giving her a long look. 'Given the right situation. *Everyone*. Even you.'

Chapter Ten

The following morning, at school, Kyle's chair was empty. Raven looked over at Brett, but Brett's eyes instantly shied away. It wasn't long before the fallout began, though. Halfway through English, Raven and Brett were summoned to the head's office. They walked in silence through the deserted corridors, and as they approached the ominous door, Brett muttered, still without looking at Raven, 'You're going to get expelled for this, you know.'

'D'you honestly think I give a damn?' Raven tossed back in reply.

But in Mr Miller's office he found Jackie, and a woman who looked like she might be Brett's mum, and Kyle's parents. Kyle was conspicuous by his absence.

Raven and Brett were directed to two empty chairs at

the end of the semicircle. Raven refused to meet Jackie's eye. The head's speech was short and brief. He gave a fairly accurate summary of what had been reported to him by the onlookers, including the bit about the picture. Kyle, apparently, was at home with bruised ribs, although his parents kept going on about how they had very nearly been broken. Mr Miller simply said that this kind of behaviour would not be tolerated in his school. All three boys would be excluded for three days, starting from now. Then it was all over and Raven and Brett went back to the classroom to fetch their things. Raven met Jackie at the gate and they drove home in silence. Raven kept waiting for her to explode, to say that this was it, this was the last straw, but when he risked a glance at her profile, he saw that she didn't even look angry. Perhaps she was actually relieved then – relieved she could phone the social worker as soon as they got home, relieved that she finally had an excuse to be rid of him.

When they got in, Raven headed straight for the stairs, but Jackie put her hand on his arm to stop him. 'If you're going to have three days off, then you may as well make yourself useful,' she said.

'What do I have to do then?' Raven asked sullenly.

'You could come and help me assemble the new TV cabinet we bought for the living room,' Jackie said. 'It arrived early this morning, flat packed of course, and Dan said he'd put it together tonight because I'm so useless at that kind of thing. But if you could help me . . .'

Raven sighed again. 'OK,' he said grudgingly.

In the living room Jackie cut open the cardboard packaging while Raven pored over the instructions. 'Oh, look at all this,' she complained as she pulled out the various-sized pieces of wood, along with the packets and packets of different-sized screws, nuts and bolts. 'These days if you buy any furniture, you need a degree in carpentry.'

'We have to start with the base,' Raven said, kneeling over the instruction sheet. 'See that long piece of wood? That's the base. Turn it over so the rubber bits are facing down.'

Jackie did as she was instructed. Then they used the electric screwdriver to secure the legs. Raven kept going back to the leaflet, telling Jackie what to do next. 'Not like that, like this,' he corrected her, turning the piece of wood the right way round.

Eventually they had built the base. Raven rocked back on his heels and surveyed it with a feeling of satisfaction. 'Well, that bit was easy,' he pronounced.

'Easy?' Jackie laughed, blowing the fringe out of her eyes. 'I'm exhausted already.'

'We can't stop now,' he said. 'We have to build the sides. Where are the small screws? The ones with the square-shaped tops?'

Jackie found them and tore the packet open with her teeth. 'I wish you'd told us,' she said indistinctly.

Raven stopped, staring down at the instructions. He didn't move.

'About the bullying,' she went on.

'Why?' Raven asked, glancing up.

'Because we could have stopped it,' she replied.

'How?' His voice was sceptical.

'By talking to the head. By talking to the parents. All schools have anti-bullying policies now. Bullies can be expelled if they are reported. But only if they are reported. Even if they hadn't been expelled, the teachers could have kept a closer eye on them, or we could have even considered moving you to a different school.'

'I don't want to change schools,' Raven said quickly. 'I don't care about Kyle and Brett any more.'

'Why? Because of Lotte?'

Raven looked back down at the instructions and said nothing.

'You really like her, don't you?' Jackie said, putting down the bag of screws.

He continued to stare down at the leaflet. 'She's all right.'

He could sense that Jackie was smiling. 'Is she your girlfriend?'

He looked up, feeling his cheeks flare. 'No!'

'OK, I was just wondering,' she said quickly.

'She's – she's just my friend,' Raven said, looking back down at the instruction sheet. 'We – we just tell each other stuff.'

'Then you're very lucky,' Jackie said. 'A really close friend, someone you can trust and really talk to, is a rare thing.'

There was a silence. 'So do I put the screws into these holes here?' Jackie asked.

'No, they go in the other side—' Raven dropped the leaflet and shuffled over to her on his knees. 'Here . . .' He guided her hand round to the other side of the piece of wood. Her hand felt warm and smooth.

'Raven?' Jackie said suddenly.

'Yeah?' He started inserting the next screw.

'D'you think one day you might be able to trust me too, the way you trust Lotte?'

Raven concentrated harder than he needed to on the tight-fitting screw. Jackie stopped helping. She was waiting for a reply.

'Dunno,' he said.

'Because you're part of the family now,' Jackie went on. 'We want you to stay with us for ever.'

'I thought you wanted to send me back,' he said, focusing on the next step of the procedure. 'That's what I overheard you saying to Dan.'

He could sense she was startled. 'When?'

'That time you were arguing in the kitchen. You said, "Perhaps we've made a mistake." '

'Oh, Raven, you overheard that?' she breathed. There was a stunned silence. He felt her hand on his arm. 'Raven, look at me,' she said.

His first instinct was to pull angrily away. But he stopped himself and raised his eyes to hers, his heart thumping.

'I wanted you. I've always wanted you. When Joyce first told us what you'd been through and showed us photos, I thought, I want him to be ours. That argument you heard between me and Dan – it was just because I was desperate. You acted as if you hated us, Raven. I thought we'd made a mistake because you seemed so unhappy here. You hardly ever spoke, you *never* smiled. I thought we'd *failed* you. I thought that living with us was making you even more unhappy.' She kept hold of his arm, her eyes locked onto his.

'I'm not unhappy here,' Raven said. 'I quite like it, actually. You're all OK, really.'

'Honestly?'

He nodded. 'So where are the small bolts that go into these slots?'

Back at school, Kyle and Brett seemed to be keeping their distance. Carlos, a boy from his class who he'd never really spoken to before, put down his lunch tray on the half-empty table across from Raven.

'How was your holiday?' he asked with a grin.

Raven glanced up and shrugged. 'Better than school at any rate.'

'It's all round the school, what you did. Served them dickheads right. They've been hassling me ever since I was made captain of the football team.'

Raven looked carefully at Carlos. 'Don't you like them either?'

'Are you kidding me? They're shitheads. No one can stand them two. It's cool that someone's finally had the guts to stand up to them. Although I never thought it would be you. You always seem to be kind of spaced out.' He laughed.

'I have things on my mind,' Raven said.

'About your mum and stuff?'

'Yeah.'

'Man, that must be tough. What are your foster parents like?'

'They're OK, I suppose,' Raven replied.

'You're lucky then. My parents can be real arseholes. Hey, d'you wanna try out for the football team on Monday? Rhys Johnson broke his arm and Mr Evans is looking for a replacement.'

Raven looked at Carlos in surprise. He'd never played much football before. But then, when they'd done ball-skills at the beginning of term, Mr Evans had said something about him being a natural goal-scorer. 'What do I have to do?' he asked.

'Just join in for a practice session next Monday. Then, at the end, Mr Evans will tell you whether you're good enough to make the team.'

The excitement that had begun to rise within him suddenly died. 'I can't,' he said. 'I've messed up my ankle.'

'Well, come along when it's better then,' Carlos replied. 'Let's go over to that table and I'll introduce you to the rest of the team.'

The sun was setting over the rooftops, the last rays stretching across the gardens, reaching in to touch the edge of his pillow. The days were getting longer. Raven sat at the end of his bed, against the wall, his knees drawn up in front of him. To his surprise, Carlos and the rest of the football lot seemed really keen for him to try out for a place on the team as soon as his ankle was better, and he sat with them regularly at lunch times now. He had been at the Russells' for nearly three months and was beginning to get used to this room, this house. Evening meals and weekends were slowly getting easier. And if he was having a bad day, he used the excuse of homework to escape to his room and Jackie seemed to be taken in, commenting more than once on his studious nature, and how she hoped that Ella would be like that when she was older.

'But it's boring,' Ella would say, rolling her eyes. 'I don't want to sit in my room studying all the time even if it meant I could be first cleverest in my class. I want to do other stuff like painting and drawing and practising for the play.'

Jackie had laughed indulgently, but Dan's eyes had met Raven's over the kitchen table and Raven had known. Dan wasn't fooled. Dan knew he went to his room to escape the family scenes, the chit-chat, the walks in Richmond Park, the board games round the kitchen table . . . All the things that reminded him that the Russells were a family. A family. Something he'd once had. Sometimes it didn't seem like such a long time ago. Sometimes, when he was sitting at his bedroom desk, in front of an empty window of black sky, all he had to do was close his eyes and he found himself back – back round the kitchen table, Mum dishing stew onto four chipped plates, the lampshade hanging low over their heads, the kitchen window fogged up with cooking steam. Sometimes it was so real he could actually taste the stew, see the rise and fall of Mum's chest beneath her red apron, hear the chink of forks on plates, breathe in the thick, foodie smell. Sometimes it left him with an ache so strong that when he opened his eyes and found himself sitting alone in his bedroom in the Russells' house, it was all he could do to stop his eyes from filling with tears. And sometimes he didn't succeed, and so sat, head propped up on his hand, watching the tears drop down onto the open page of his exercise book, smudging the ink and puckering the paper.

On one such evening there was a knock on the door and Dan came in. Raven glanced up at him and then quickly turned his head away, brushing the side of his hand swiftly across his cheeks. He heard the sound of the door closing and the creak of springs as Dan sat down on the edge of the bed.

'You all right, buddy?' Dan asked.

Raven hesitated and then thought it best not to answer. Perhaps if he just ignored him, Dan would get the hint and leave him alone.

'Call me an old fusspot but I'm a bit worried about you.'

Raven turned his gaze back to the window.

Suddenly Dan's hand was on his shoulder. 'What's going on, old man?'

Outside, a pale pink sunset was spreading itself across the sky. If he concentrated hard enough, he felt as if he could lift himself out of this room, away from Dan and his ingenuous concern, and into the sky.

'If you talk to me . . .' Dan began. 'It might – it might help.'

How? Raven wanted to ask. How on earth would it help? Would Dan somehow be able to pierce his bubble of loneliness and allow him to step back into the living world? The living world where people talked and worked and played and did things just for the sake of doing them, just for fun. Where people laughed at things on TV, chatted for the sake of chatting, and weren't haunted by thoughts of a lost past and a hopeless future.

He blinked and felt a tear escape down the side of his nose. He pressed the heels of his hands to his eyes.

And Dan just sat quietly beside him, rubbing Raven's back, appearing to realize that words couldn't make a difference any more.

A blanket of geese rose from the lake and flew in a wide arc towards the horizon. Spring had crept up on them and the air was almost balmy. Dan and Ella were frightening the deer, rushing about in a game of 'it'. Ella was screeching now, and Dan caught up with her, reached out and swept her off the ground. He hoisted her over his shoulder and she began kicking her legs, still screeching. Jackie moved in slightly towards Raven as they walked. Her arm brushed against his. And then suddenly she put her arm round his shoulders. Raven could feel the touch of her fingers against the top of his arm.

'It's a beautiful day, isn't it?' she said to him.

Raven nodded.

'How are things going for you at school?' she asked him.

He shrugged. 'Better. I'm trying out for the football team on Monday.'

'Really?' She pulled away to look at him, her face lit up with pleasure.

He nodded.

'That's brilliant, lovey. I'm sure you'll make the team. And what about Kyle and Brett? Have they backed off at long last?'

'Yeah, they avoid me now.' He gave a short laugh. 'I think they're scared of me.'

Jackie smiled. 'Bullies tend to be cowards. That's why they pick on people. To try and make themselves feel better.'

There was a silence. It felt strange, walking with Jackie's arm around his shoulders. But just for now he didn't feel like pulling away.

'I know I've said this before, but how about inviting Lotte back to dinner after school sometime this week?' Jackie asked.

He smiled. 'OK.'

On Monday afternoon Raven boarded the bus, hot and sweaty from the football game. As he made his way to the top deck, he spotted Lotte's fair head; she was sitting at the front with her feet up.

'Hi,' he said. 'Why are you going home so late?'

She looked up, smiling in surprise. 'Piano lesson. Did you make the team?'

'Dunno yet. Evans is a slave-driver. But I scored two goals, anyway.'

She let out a puff of air. 'Then you're bound to have made it. That's more than the team's scored at any match this year.'

Revved up by her confidence in him, Raven suddenly had an idea. 'Let's *do* something before we go home. I know, let's write a letter to Steve. Something like: *We know what you did to Anna*. Then we can post it through his letter box, ring the bell and watch through the binoculars from the empty house. He'll be scared shitless.'

'Now?' Lotte looked uncertain.

'Why not?' Raven said, managing to sound more off-hand than he felt. 'Watching Steve freak out over our letter will be more fun than doing homework.'

Lotte checked her watch. 'It's late.'

Raven reached into his bag and pulled out his mobile phone. 'We'll call now and say we're doing our homework in the library.'

Lotte hesitated. 'Don't you think you're getting a bit obsessed by this whole thing? Spying on him, sending him letters . . .'

'Wouldn't you be obsessed if you knew the man who'd killed your mum was walking around, leading a normal life, while your life had been *ruined*—?' Suddenly he was almost shouting.

'OK, OK.' She cut him off quickly. 'I'm sorry. You're

right, we should do something. But what if he sees us delivering the letter?'

'We'll be quick. It's unlikely.'

'Yes, but what if he does? Then he'll know we know. He may grab Billy and leave town or something.'

'Look, do you want to or not?' Raven snapped. 'We're going to have to take some risks if we want to scare him, you know. Otherwise we can just sit back and let the bastard carry on with his life.'

'No, OK, I want to do it.' Lotte's eyes shone. 'Are we really going to write that? He's going to be so spooked!'

Raven smiled.

They got off the bus at the next stop and headed back up to the tube station. When they reached Hounslow, they made straight for the boarded-up house, and in the late afternoon sunlight slanting across the dusty floor they sat down cross-legged. Raven pulled his pencil case and exercise book out of his school bag. Carefully ripping out a page, he handed it to Lotte. 'It's better if you write it.'

'OK.' She uncapped a biro. 'What shall I write?'

'Write it in red,' Raven said, handing her a felt-tip. 'Write it in capitals.'

'OK. What?'

'WE KNOW WHAT YOU DID TO ANNA. That's it. Short and sharp. Leave the rest to his imagination.'

Lotte got to work, the tip of her tongue touching her top lip. Raven examined her handiwork with approval. It was neat but bold.

'We haven't got an envelope,' she said.

'Doesn't matter,' Raven replied, folding the paper into quarters. 'Here. Write STEVE WINCHAM on it.'

She did as instructed.

'OK. It's better if only one of us delivers it, so I'll go. You stay here with the binoculars.'

'But Steve knows you,' Lotte countered. 'If anyone spots you and Steve asks around, he might realize it was you who delivered it. Whereas he's only met me once. If he sees me again, he probably won't recognize me. And if I get caught, I can say that I'm just the carrier. That I was paid to deliver the note or something.'

It made sense. 'Yeah, OK,' Raven agreed reluctantly.

She picked up the folded letter, her eyes bright. 'So I just put it through the letter box and then run?'

'Yes. But ring Steve's buzzer too, so that he comes down and sees it. We can't risk it lying on the doormat all night.'

'What if he looks out of the window and sees me?' Lotte worried.

'Don't come straight back here. Go round the block. Walk fast but don't run. Then, when you're sure you're not being followed, come back here. Meanwhile I'll watch Steve through the binoculars.'

Lotte stood up. 'OK. Now?'

'Now,' Raven answered.

She took a deep breath and went downstairs.

Raven watched through the binoculars as Lotte crossed over the road and, glancing nervously up and down the street, hurried up the steps to the front door of the block of flats. She hesitated, looked over her shoulder, and then, in one quick motion, posted the paper through the letter box. Next she turned round and, with an anxious glance up at Raven's window, went back down the steps, pausing at the edge of the pavement to let a white van pass. Raven fought against the urge to throw open the window in front of him and shout down. In her nervous state she had totally forgotten to ring Steve's bell.

He watched helplessly as Lotte crossed the road and began to make her way quickly down the street. Then suddenly she stopped and turned to look back the way she had come. After a moment of hesitation, she hurried back across the road, breaking into a jog and heading towards the front door again. When she reached it, she quickly examined the row of buzzers and then pressed her thumb against the top one.

She had gone back down the steps and had just stepped onto the pavement when Raven saw her suddenly whirl round. He jerked the binoculars up in alarm, only to catch a view of grey sky. Lowering them, he saw in horror that Steve was now standing there in the doorway, the open paper in his hand. Lotte began to run.

There was an angry shout from the street below and Raven dropped the binoculars to the floor and hurtled down the stairs. He found the gap in the board and thrust himself outside. As he ran out of the garden and emerged into the street, he saw Steve disappearing round the corner of the block. Sprinting down the alley between two houses that he remembered backed onto the high street, Raven jumped up onto the wheelie-bins at the end and swung himself over the high wooden fence, landing on the pavement the other side. A moment of panic, then to his relief he caught sight of Lotte's flying blonde hair about fifty metres ahead of him as she dodged the crowds through the high street. Without stopping to see where Steve was, Raven pounded after her. He didn't catch up with her until she had nearly reached the mouth of the tube station.

She lashed out at him and almost sent him flying as he grabbed her arm.

'No – no – it's me!'

She let out a squawk of surprise but was too breathless to reply, her face puce, her eyes wide with fright.

'No – not the tube station – he'll catch us on the platform . . .' Raven gasped with difficulty.

'Where then?' Her voice was desperate.

'This way – this way – follow me!'

Raven veered off the high street and through the park gates, Lotte at his heels, their shoes slapping loudly against the concrete path. An old lady sitting on a bench squinted up at them with interest as they came tearing past. Some way ahead of them, a man could be seen slowly walking his dog.

'Stop them!' came a shout from behind. 'Stop those kids!'

The man wheeled round in surprise. He dropped his dog's leash and started walking rapidly towards Lotte and Raven. They instantly split away from each other, giving the man a wide berth. Then Lotte suddenly began to slow, clutching her side.

Raven caught up with her, grabbing her by the arm. He allowed himself a quick glance over his shoulder and saw that Steve was gaining.

'Keep going!' he begged her.

'No, I can't – it hurts too much! You go!' She tried to disengage her hand from his grasp.

He tightened his grip. 'Come on!' he shouted at her. 'We're nearly there!'

They made it to the edge of the wood and dived in between the trees. Within moments the undergrowth was thick around their legs, the tall grass tickling the backs of their knees. They waded in as far as they could and then Raven whispered, 'Lie down – lie down here now!'

Lotte needed no prompting. They both threw themselves to the ground amid the stinging nettles and the tangled vines and ivy, and tried to muffle their breathing, their hands over their mouths.

When the pounding in his ears and gasping in his throat finally began to recede, Raven was aware of a new sound – the twittering of sparrows. There were some distant cries from the football pitch at the far end of the park. The sound of branches moving in the wind. And apart from that, complete silence. No crunching of twigs underfoot. No giveaway sounds from their pursuer. Nothing.

Lotte slowly raised her head. Wisps of hair stuck to her damp forehead and the colour was still high in her cheeks. A small twig and a curled green leaf adorned her hair. 'D'you think we've lost him?'

Raven raised himself cautiously onto his elbows, scouring the thick, gnarled tree trunks that surrounded them. 'Maybe. Let's just give it another minute.'

They did, scouring the trees around them in the diminishing light.

They sat up slowly, facing each other cross-legged in the tall grass, brushing bits of leaves from their hair. Lotte glanced around, nervous, skittish as a deer.

'It's all right,' Raven said. 'He's given up and gone home, I'm sure.'

'Do you think he recognized us?' Lotte asked him, her voice still a whisper.

'Nah,' he said with more confidence than he felt. 'He only saw the backs of our heads.'

'But he would have seen my face – I turned round when I heard his front door open.'

'But he only met you once,' Raven countered. 'I doubt he'd have remembered your face.'

'Thanks a lot!' Lotte exclaimed.

He looked at her. And smiled with relief. They both began to laugh.

'You look like something out of *A Midsummer Night's Dream*,' he told her.

She rolled her eyes and pulled the remaining leaf from her hair. 'That was a close shave.'

'You're telling me.'

'All because I forgot to ring Steve's buzzer. But he must have been standing right behind the front door to have read the letter so quickly.'

'Yeah, talk about bad timing. He must have been in the hallway, about to go out or something.'

'How did you catch me up so fast?' Lotte wanted to know.

'There was a short cut between the houses. I was sure you'd be running for the tube station.'

'And I would have gone into it if you hadn't come. I was somehow hoping there might be a train there waiting.'

'And if there hadn't been? Steve would have caught you easily on the platform.'

She looked at him. The pale evening light slanted through the branches of the trees. 'Why did you come after me? We could have both been caught,' Lotte said.

'I wasn't about to let you get caught on your own,' Raven replied.

Chapter Eleven

'I've got a plan,' he said to Lotte in the playground the next day.

'Of how to extract a confession from Steve?' She looked at him, her expression suddenly nervous.

He nodded. 'D'you want to come to my house after school?'

'Yes, but hold on. I don't know if we should do this on our own. Steve knows what I look like now. He so nearly caught us yesterday! And what if he calls the police again?'

Raven narrowed his eyes at her in annoyance. 'The police can't do anything to us, we're minors,' he retorted. 'Anyway, I thought you said you wanted an adventure. If you're too chicken—'

'Hold on, hold on,' Lotte interrupted quickly. 'I didn't say I wouldn't do it. I'll come over and listen to your plan.

But it had better be a good one because otherwise—'

'It's foolproof,' Raven retorted, and walked away.

Jackie was delighted. She picked them all up from school and they piled into the back of the car with Ella. Ella was having a sulk, her finger in her mouth. She hadn't been made star of the day. 'Lucy was star of the day *again*,' she said bitterly. 'Miss Mann always chooses her to be star of the day. She's just a teacher's pet, that's all.'

'What shall we have for supper, Ella?' Jackie asked, trying to distract her.

'I was never given any stars when I was in Year One,' Lotte said to her cheerfully. 'I was always Lotte Loud-mouth, the kid who never stopped talking.'

'That sounds familiar!' Jackie laughed.

'Did you get Choosing Time when you were in Year One?' Ella asked Lotte, removing her finger from her mouth like a stopper.

'Yeah, I think so . . .'

'We have it on Friday afternoons after library,' Ella said. 'I always choose to play with the dollies. That's my favourite. What did you play with?'

'Er – the Lego, I think.' Lotte shot Raven a grin.

'Yuk!' Ella laughed. 'Lego is for boys!'

'Well, I always was a bit of a tomboy,' Lotte smiled.

After a fish and chip supper Ella would not leave them alone. She stood outside Raven's bedroom door, knocking and knocking.

'We're busy!' Raven shouted to her.

'I wanna see what you're doing!'

'Homework! Go away!'

'Can I do my colouring with you?'

'No!'

Ella began to wail and Jackie's voice sounded on the stairs. 'Hey, Ella, why don't you and I make some cupcakes that we can give to Lotte and Raven when they've finished their homework?'

Lotte was looking around Raven's room, picking up his library books, looking through his CDs, fingering the top of the silver frame that held his favourite photo. His mother was wearing a wide-brimmed straw hat and was holding him on her knee. She was laughing at the camera, her chin raised. He was staring into the lens, frowning. It had been taken in their garden, one hot summer's day a long time ago. 'She's pretty,' Lotte said. 'You look a lot like her. Except for your eyes—' She broke off suddenly. 'Hey,' she said.

'What?'

'In this photo you look a lot like – like some other kid I've seen . . .'

'All kids look the same at that age.' Raven turned away and sat down cross-legged at the end of his bed. 'Right, are we going to start formulating our plan, then?' He smiled slightly. 'I'm going to borrow Dan's camcorder,' he went on. 'He hardly ever uses it so he shouldn't notice if it goes missing for one day. I already fiddled about with it when he was out once and it's pretty simple to use and so small it'll fit into my coat pocket. You'll go into the empty house and wait for me on the second floor, as far away as possible from the entrance but where the windows are still boarded up. I'm going to go to Steve's flat and ring the bell. When he opens, I'm going to say that you and I were playing around in the empty house and that you slipped and twisted your ankle. I'll say that you can't even stand. I'll ask him to come in and carry you down the stairs.'

Lotte was kneeling on the end of the bed, chewing her thumbnail thoughtfully. 'And then?'

'And then, when he comes, I'll lead him upstairs, sit him down and tell him I want to talk to him.'

'But won't he get angry?' Lotte asked. 'When he sees that it was just a hoax, won't he just march out again?'

'If I tell him I've got something important to say, he'll listen,' Raven said. 'Believe me. And then I'll tell him that

I know what happened. I'll tell him I actually saw him push and kill my mum. I'll tell him that it's no use pretending any more, that I won't tell anyone, as long as he admits it to me. Then all the while you'll be hiding in one of those empty crates, filming him secretly with the camcorder.'

Lotte looked dubious. 'D'you really think he'd confess just like that, after all this time?'

Raven gave her a steady look. 'I can be very persuasive.'

Lotte looked uncomfortable. 'What d'you mean? You're going to threaten him? I don't want to be involved if it's going to turn nasty, you know.'

'I'll *persuade* him,' he said, carefully holding her gaze.

Lotte started biting her thumbnail again. 'Really? Just with words? What if he gets angry? What if he tries to murder *us*?'

'He won't even see you. You'll be hiding in the crate the whole time! There's no way he'll ever guess that you're in there!'

'He might do something to you,' Lotte said. 'He might get really angry, especially if he thinks you're going to go to the police.'

'I'll tell him straight away that I'm not going to do that. He thinks I like him. He's known me a long time. He'll trust me, you'll see.'

She held his gaze a moment longer, as if searching his eyes for the truth. Then she said, 'OK. But you'll have to show me exactly what you want me to do. And we'll have to go and check out the empty house and make sure one of those crates upstairs is big enough for me to fit in, and—' Lotte cupped her hands over her mouth. 'Shit, I'm so nervous already! I can't wait for it all to be over.'

Raven was silent for a moment, looking at her.

She looked at him. 'What?'

He shrugged. 'Nothing.'

'You and Lotte are going to the cinema this Friday, after school?' Jackie sounded pleased. She smiled at Dan across the table. 'That sounds like fun. What time shall I pick you up?'

Dan grinned at her. 'That's not very cool, sweetheart. I'm sure Raven would prefer to make his own way back.'

Raven nodded.

'Can I come?' Ella asked optimistically.

'After the film you'll come straight home?' Jackie went on.

'Well, I think Lotte wants to go to McDonald's. But I won't be late,' Raven said.

'McDonald's? Yum! I *love* McDonald's!' Ella cried.

'Let's say nine,' Dan said. 'Make absolutely sure you're

home by nine at the latest or we'll be sending out the search parties.' But he was beaming.

'So what are the two of you going to see?' Jackie asked.

Raven hesitated, feeling his mind go blank. 'The um – the – the . . .'

'*The Rat Catcher*?' Ella suggested helpfully.

'Yeah, that's it. *The Rat Catcher*.'

'Oh, not fair!' she wailed.

'Well, maybe Daddy can take you to see it next week,' Jackie said.

Raven let his breath out slowly and picked up his fork again.

'Did you ask?' He went up to Lotte at break the next morning.

'They said yes. I told them it was someone's birthday party.' Lotte glanced at Alice, who was listening intently. 'Can I just talk to Raven for a moment in private?'

Alice flounced off with a roll of her eyes.

Lotte said, 'Shall we meet at the tube station after school?'

'Yes.'

'OK, cool!' Lotte brought her hands to her mouth. 'Shit, I can't believe we're actually going to do this!'

* * *

'Book!' Ella yelled.

'Seven words!' Jackie cried out, reading Dan's signs. 'Goodness, that's a lot! First word: *The*.'

Dan got down on his hands and knees on the living-room carpet and began to paw the ground and growl.

'Dog!' Ella yelled.

Dan shook his head and bared his teeth and pretended to maul a cushion.

Ella screamed with laughter.

'Oh, Dan, do be careful, that's the cushion Mother gave me.'

Dan sat back on his haunches and let out a terrifying roar.

'Lion,' Raven said, beginning to laugh.

Dan nodded enthusiastically, still growling.

'Oh, clever Raven, clever Raven!' Ella shouted gleefully, patting him on the back.

'Next word: *the*,' Jackie said.

Dan got up, hurried into the kitchen and came back riding the broom.

'Wizard!' Ella screeched. '*Harry Potter! Harry Potter!* I win!'

'Hold on, darling, it's: *The Lion, the*—' Jackie put her arms out to restrain Ella as she leaped forward off the couch to take centre stage in the middle of the living-room floor.

Dan, still astride his broomstick, began to cackle loudly.

'Witch!' Ella shrieked. 'It's a witch, isn't it, Daddy?'

Dan nodded, grinning, and held up five fingers.

'I know!' Raven jumped up. *'The Lion, the Witch and the*—' He suddenly stopped himself and turned to Ella expectantly. After a brief moment of wide-eyed hesitation, her eyes suddenly lit up. *'The Lion, the Witch and the Wardrobe!'* she shrieked, leaping up and down. 'I win! I win! I win!'

Raven sat down again.

'Clever Ella Bella!' Dan applauded loudly and came to sit on the arm of the sofa as Ella danced to the centre of the living room. 'OK, now think carefully. Remember to choose something short that is easy to mime . . .'

Jackie put her arm round Raven's shoulders and gave him a squeeze. 'That was sweet of you,' she said quietly.

Chapter Twelve

What did it take to kill a person? To be a murderer? It was such a strong word. One that conjured up images of evil men with gimlet eyes, of court cases and prison cells, of newspapers and newsreaders. A murderer would start out like the rest of us. Thinking there would never come a time when they would take another's life. Never imagining themselves in a situation where they would grab a gun, or a knife, or a bomb. In relatively peaceful England it was hardly something you would aspire to as you grew up. But then, one day, something would happen, something you had never imagined, something that would lead to another person's death. Ordinary people could become killers. Anyone could kill another person. It really wasn't so difficult after all.

Propped against the pillows, Raven watched the

bluish dawn spread across the sky. It was going to be a beautiful day. The clouds on the horizon were tinged with gold. The other houses were still sleeping, their windows dark, curtains drawn. The roads were still quiet, the birds were twittering in the trees and the day had only just begun. By the time the sun set again at the end of this day, something momentous would have happened. Steve would have confessed to the killing and everything would have fallen into its proper place. The scrambled thoughts inside his head would cease. The red-hot anger in his chest would cool. Everything would be as it should be. Everything would start to make sense. The nightmare would be over. The story would have its proper ending.

He felt nervous, but it was a good feeling. It made him feel alive. The plan was very simple. He felt sure it would not fail. Getting through the school day would be the hardest bit. Knowing what was waiting for him at the end of it – Steve's confession – his own absolution. Freedom. It was only hours away.

At breakfast everyone was chatty, talking about the weekend. Ella wanted to go to the zoo. Dan wanted to drive out into the countryside. Jackie wanted to visit the Science Museum. Raven smiled serenely at them all. He didn't mind what they did. After today everything would be fine. After today he would chat and laugh and join in with them. Everything would be different. As he left the house with Jackie and Ella, the camcorder safely hidden away at the bottom of his school bag, he felt almost jubilant. Dan gave him his usual squeeze on the shoulder and said, 'Have fun tonight.'

Raven smiled his thanks.

In the car Jackie was testing Ella on her five times table. When she got stuck, Ella turned to look at Raven, who mouthed her the answers.

'Gosh, you've really got the hang of your five times table!' Jackie exclaimed.

'I know!' Ella crowed, darting Raven a triumphant smile.

At the gate Jackie gave Raven a pat on the shoulder as Ella charged off to meet her friends. 'I'll see you tonight at nine at the latest,' she said to him with a smile. 'You will be back by nine, Raven, won't you?' Despite her smile, she sounded genuinely anxious.

'Yes,' he said, and meant it.

She kissed the top of his head and waved him goodbye.

In English Lotte kept shooting him furtive, wide-eyed

glances. Her cheeks were flushed and she looked nervous and excited. Raven had been afraid that she might have changed her mind but she looked as enthusiastic as ever. At lunch time he received such a vigorous slap on the back that it almost sent him face down into his plate of shepherd's pie.

'Yo, dude!' It was Carlos, his face beaming.

'What?'

'Haven't your heard? You made the team. Your name's up on the notice board!' Carlos held up his hand for a high-five. 'See, I told you,' he declared to the rest of the table. 'I told you I'd find a player even better than Johnson!' He held out his hands, palms up. 'Was I right or was I right?'

People reached over to high-five Raven or punch him in the shoulder. He grinned back at them, bemused, his face flushed with pleasure.

But back in class, time seemed to stand still. Raven tried to keep his eyes from locking onto the classroom clock. But as the afternoon wore on, he could feel his heart-rate picking up. Lotte seemed on tenterhooks too and got told off twice for talking. When the final bell went, it was all Raven could do to keep himself from jumping out of his chair.

There was the usual mayhem and clatter as everyone

scraped back their chairs, packed up their bags and headed out into the hall. Raven kept a careful eye out for Lotte, making sure that he didn't leave the classroom at the same time as she did. The corridors resounded with home-time excitement and early weekend cheer. He made his way through the crowd at the gate, down the street towards the tube station.

When they arrived at the boarded-up house, they got to work, pulling away the rest of the boarding until the whole of the window was cleared. Then they climbed through easily. Inside, Raven led Lotte up to the second-floor room, the one he had singled out for its rusty key in the door. It was a big, L-shaped space with creaking floorboards, a scratched wooden dining table and two broken chairs. The two boarded-up windows let in a faint glow of bluish late-afternoon light. Dan's powerful torch was where he had left it, on the table. He switched it on and it created a warm golden puddle on the floorboards. Raven got Lotte to help him drag the biggest crate down the stairs and into the corner of the room. They set it on its side against the wall and Lotte climbed in gingerly. 'Ew!' she squealed.

'What?'

'Cobwebs. Oh, gross. I bet there are tons of spiders in here!'

Raven took his penknife out of his pocket and set about widening one of the cracks. 'You'll have to hold the camera lens in between this crack here. It only needs to be a few centimetres wide. You'll be able to zoom and stuff and make sure Steve's face is clearly visible.'

'What if the battery runs out or something?' Lotte asked, beginning to giggle.

'It won't. I've fully charged it and it's all working properly. It's on auto-focus, so all you'll have to do is keep your eye against the viewfinder and make sure that Steve's in the frame,' Raven said. He got the crack wide enough to accommodate the camcorder's lens. Then he patiently showed Lotte how to record. They did a couple of trial runs with Raven sitting on one of the broken chairs at the table, pretending to be Steve.

'The important thing is to make sure that you can see the REC sign in the viewfinder at all times, and that Steve's face is in the frame. And try to keep the camcorder as still as possible. I'll try and position Steve so he's sitting here, like this, facing you . . . OK, enough practice or we'll wear the battery down. Let's see what you've done.'

Lotte climbed out of the crate and handed him the camcorder and he switched it to PLAYBACK to watch what she'd filmed.

'Is it OK?' she asked anxiously, peering over his shoulder.

'It's fine. A bit wobbly, but fine.' He rewound the tape and handed it back to her. 'When you get into the crate, make sure you're sitting comfortably so that you don't need to move once we've come in. Prop your elbows on your knees so your arms don't start to ache. And keep your thumb on the record button the whole time, but whatever you do, don't press it again unless the REC sign disappears.'

She nodded intently, drawing her lower lip in between her teeth.

'OK,' he said. 'I think we're ready.'

Lotte stared at him in the strange light. 'Really?' she asked, her voice suddenly faint.

Raven nodded.

She took a deep breath and let it out slowly. 'Jesus, my heart's really thumping. What if it doesn't work? What if he won't come in?'

'He'll come in,' Raven assured her.

'What if he guesses someone's in the crate, filming him?'

'He won't. Why on earth would he?'

Lotte sucked in her breath. Her eyes looked huge. 'I hope you're right. Oh God, Raven, I'm feeling really scared!'

'You don't have to do anything. You never have to emerge from the crate. If the worst comes to the worst, he'll just storm out. He'd never know you were here.'

'OK, OK,' Lotte said desperately. 'But do me one favour, Raven, just try and get him to confess quickly.'

'I'll do my best.'

She held out her hand. 'Good luck.'

Raven shook her hand and stood still, looking at her.

'What?' she said with a smile.

He hesitated, his breath threatening to catch in his throat. 'When this is over, are you – are we still going to – you know . . . ?'

'What?'

'Be friends?' he said in a rush.

She raised her eyebrows in surprise. 'Of course.'

He regarded her doubtfully, chewing his lip.

'Are you scared?' Lotte asked him.

'Nah . . . well, kind of . . .'

'It'll be OK,' she said. 'Even if it doesn't work, at least we'll have tried.'

'Yeah.' His mouth was dry. He suddenly knew that, after this, nothing was ever going to be the same. What excuse would he have to go up to Lotte in the playground? Where would they sneak off to after school once their hiding place was discovered? What stories would he have left to tell her to make her dance from foot to foot?

'Here goes.' With one last wide-eyed look at him, Lotte turned and climbed into the crate. Raven pushed it back against the wall and kicked it a few times to check it was stable. 'Have you got the camcorder?' he called to her.

'Yes!'

'OK, I'm off!'

It was all frighteningly simple. Lotte and the camera were set. The key was in the door. He would close it and lock it quietly as soon as Steve stepped into the room. Hopefully Steve wouldn't even notice. Now all he had to do was persuade him to come. He hurried down the stairs and back into the evening light. He checked his watch. They still had plenty of time. The Russells wouldn't be expecting him home for hours and Steve would have fetched Billy home from school ages ago. Raven crossed the empty road over to Steve's block of flats. He put his finger to the buzzer, took a deep breath and pressed.

There was a long silence. Raven was aware for the first time of the thudding of his heart. His legs suddenly felt weak. This was the moment he had been waiting for. Ever since she had died. Two whole years ago. Steve deserved it. He really did.

'Yes?' came the voice.

'It's Raven.'

'Raven! What a surprise! Are the Russells—?'

'Come down quickly. Please, it's really urgent.'

Silence. Then a thudding from the stairs. The door opened. Steve was in his slippers. 'Are you here on your own again? Where are the—?'

'I need your help.'

'Does Joyce know you're here?'

'It's my friend. The one you met. Lotte. We climbed into that deserted house across the road to explore and she fell down the stairs and sprained her ankle. She can't walk. She can't get out . . .'

Steve was looking at him incredulously. 'What on earth—? You broke into that house? When?'

'Today. It was just for fun. Just to explore.'

'Raven, what the hell are you doing messing about here? Where are the Russells?'

'Can you just come and help her? She's really hurt—'

'This is just typical of social services,' Steve snapped. 'Letting you run around like— OK, fine, wait here while I go get my keys.'

He disappeared. Raven waited. Stared up at the blind windows of the second floor. Get ready, Lotte, we're coming . . .

Steve came back out of the door. He was holding Billy by the hand. The little boy was wearing dungarees and had traces of chocolate round his mouth. 'Daddy, where are we going?' He looked at Raven in surprise. 'Have you come to play?'

Raven glared at Steve. 'Why are you bringing Billy?'

'I can't leave him on his own,' Steve said.

As they reached the window at the back of the house, Steve peered in. 'What did you want to go in there for? This is serious stuff, Raven – this is breaking and entering, and it could be dangerous: this house is very old—'

Raven ignored him and climbed through the window. 'She's upstairs,' he said.

Steve picked Billy up and climbed awkwardly over the sill. They went up the stairs slowly, deliberately, Raven hoping to warn Lotte of their imminent arrival. Steve sneezed loudly and Billy asked chirpily, 'Daddy, why is Raven taking us into this yukky house?'

'Because he's gone and done something silly . . .'

Steve walked ahead into the L-shaped room. Raven closed the door behind him, in one swift movement turning the key in the lock and slipping it into his pocket. Steve advanced to the middle of the room, Billy by his side, and looked around in surprise at the table and chairs, the old crate and the torch. 'Where's your friend?'

'She's not here.'

Steve turned towards Raven. 'Is this some kind of practical joke? Raven, I really haven't got time for this—'

'Have a seat,' Raven said.

Steve looked at him in amazement. 'What for?'

'I need to talk to you.'

'Here? Couldn't we talk in the flat?'

'It's better here.'

Reluctantly Steve sat down on one of the wooden chairs. 'Look,' he began, 'if the Russells don't know you're here, then I suggest we go back to the flat and call them, or I'll have Joyce on my case again—'

'It's fine. This won't take long,' Raven said.

Billy held out his arms and charged round the room, pretending to be an aeroplane.

'What is it, Raven?' Steve asked.

Raven took the other chair with his back to the crate, forcing Steve to turn slightly to face him. 'I want you to tell me what really happened to my mum.'

'What happened to Mum?' Steve stared at him, incredulous. 'But you know what happened, Raven. It will only upset you. Why d'you want to go over it all again?'

'Because I know.'

'Know what?'

'Who killed her.'

'Raven, it was an accident. We've been over this so many times. The therapist has been through it with you again and again. It was an accident. Nobody killed her.'

'You're lying!'

'Raven, why are you starting on this again?'

Billy crawled out from beneath the table. 'Daddy, can we go home now? I don't like it here.'

'Just a minute, Billy . . .' Steve's eyes didn't leave Raven's face. 'What's brought all this on again? Have you been talking about it with the Russells? Are you seeing a new therapist?'

'Daddy?'

'Be quiet, Billy—'

'I'm not seeing any psychiatrists any more!' Raven snapped. 'This has got nothing to do with anybody else! I just want to know—'

'Daddy?'

'Billy, will you just—?'

'Daddy, there's a person in here.'

Billy had got round to the back of the crate and was peering into the gap between the crate and the wall. The gap that Lotte had slipped into, only minutes before . . .

Raven jumped up. 'Get away from there!' he shouted.

'It's a girl!' Billy announced gleefully. 'I think she's spying on us!'

Raven lunged at Billy just as Steve started to get to his feet. Billy gave a yelp as Raven grabbed him by the arm and Steve yelled, 'Be gentle with your brother!'

Then Lotte emerged from behind the crate, her tie askew, her white shirt streaked with dirt. 'I – I'm sorry,' she stammered to Steve. 'I – we were just playing a game.' Her cheeks were flaming pink and she kept the camcorder hidden behind her back.

'Are you a spy?' Billy asked her.

Steve gaped at her. 'Now look here, what the hell's going on? Are you two having a laugh?' His eyes narrowed suddenly. 'Have you really twisted your ankle or is this your idea of a joke?'

'I – I haven't twisted my ankle,' Lotte stuttered. 'We – we were just playing a game, that's all.'

'Right, well, that's enough messing around in here.' Steve strode over to the door. 'You can both come back to the flat and have a chat with me like civilized people.' He gave the door handle an angry rattle. 'Oh, for fuck sake. This door is stuck!'

'No it's not, it's locked,' Raven said.

Lotte stepped back against the wall, her eyes wide. Billy had turned the crate over and climbed inside it.

'Well, unlock it then!' Steve shouted.

'No,' Raven said.

Lotte glanced nervously from Raven to Steve. 'Perhaps you should, Raven,' she said in a small voice. 'It's – it's not really going to work now . . .'

She was talking about the camcorder, and the plan to film the confession. But a confession was a confession, even if it wasn't recorded, and Lotte would be a witness. They had come too far now. He wasn't going to give up so easily.

'What's not going to work? Raven, give me the key right now,' Steve said, his voice rising.

'No,' Raven said again.

Steve stared at him. 'Why?'

'Because I want you to tell me the truth—'

'What truth?' Steve shouted.

'Look, we know what you did,' Lotte said in a rush. Her eyes were wild, but her expression was defiant. 'We just want you to tell us yourself. We just want you to confess.'

'What the hell do you kids want me to confess to?' Steve gaped at them both. 'You're as barmy as each other! Is this supposed to be some kind of joke?'

'It's not a joke.' Lotte's voice was steady but her eyes betrayed her apparent calm. 'We know what you did to Raven's mum.'

Steve stopped suddenly. A strange look came over his face. He turned to Raven. 'Is that what you're telling people now?' he said slowly. 'That I *killed* her?'

Raven didn't move. It hurt to breathe. All he had wanted was for Steve to confess.

Steve turned back to Lotte. 'Look,' he began. 'I'm sorry, but I never killed my wife. I don't know what Raven's been telling you but he's not well. He hasn't been well for a long—'

'It's not your wife we're talking about,' Lotte interrupted. 'It's Raven's mum!'

Steve stared at her, then quietly said, 'But Raven's mother *was* my wife.'

There was a sudden silence. Even Billy stopped making car noises and sat in the overturned crate, looking from one face to another. Then Lotte turned to Raven, her face white. 'What's he talking about?' she breathed.

'Ignore him,' Raven said coldly. 'He's mad.'

Steve sat down on the chair, elbows on his knees, rubbing his eyes. 'Look,' he said slowly, 'Raven, you're not well. Remember, that's one of the reasons you had to go away—'

'Why are you pretending Raven's mother was your wife?' Lotte asked him angrily.

Steve turned to her incredulously. 'Because she *was!*'

'When did you marry her?' Lotte faltered.

'When?' Steve's eyes were bulging again. 'Fifteen years ago in Cork. Raven was born there, but we didn't have Billy till we came to London.'

Lotte froze. The colour left her face. She stared at Steve. Then she stared at Raven.

'He's lying,' Raven said.

'But – but why – why would he?' Lotte stammered.

Steve was staring at Raven. 'What have you been telling people, Raven? That I killed Mum? That I'm not really your dad?'

Lotte slid to a squatting position against the wall, her eyes huge in her face. 'Oh my God,' she breathed. 'Oh my God, oh my God – he's your dad? Steve's actually your *dad?*'

'He's lying!' Raven cried savagely. 'He's not my father! He was never my father!'

Lotte turned to look at Raven, searching for re-assurance. 'Then why? Why is he saying this?' Her voice was imploring. Suddenly she sprang to her feet and crossed the room to where their blazers lay tossed on top of their school bags.

'He's out of his mind,' Raven said icily. 'He's just telling stories to try and buy himself time.'

Lotte grabbed Raven's blazer.

'He's just trying to frighten you off,' Raven persisted.

Lotte made a choking sound. Raven and Steve both turned to look at her at the same time. Raven's blazer dangled from her outstretched arm. 'If Steve's not your father' – her voice caught in a whimper – 'then why does it say Raven *Wincham* on the name tag of your blazer?'

'Give that to me!' Raven strode across the room and snatched the blazer out of Lotte's hand. Then he ripped the name tag out of the collar and threw it on the floor. 'I'm not Raven Wincham,' he spat at Steve. 'I'm Raven Winter. You're not my father. I never knew my father. You're just the man who killed my mother.'

'The photo in your room . . .' Lotte said slowly. 'That's why you reminded me of someone . . . Billy. You're Billy's brother. Billy's actually your brother . . . Oh my God . . .' Her voice shook.

Steve started towards Raven, his hand outstretched. 'Give me the key right now. We're going back to the flat and I'm calling Joyce—'

Raven picked up a jagged piece of glass from the floor by the window and held it out in front of him. Steve and Lotte froze.

There was a whimper from the crate-boat and a voice said, 'Daddy, why is Raven shouting again?'

'You're scaring your brother,' Steve said softly, sitting back down. 'Why don't you let Lotte and Billy get out of here and go and entertain themselves in the flat for a while? Then you and me can have a proper talk.'

Raven said nothing. He needed space to think. At the side of the room, Lotte had slid back down the wall, her white school shirt hanging untidily over her grey skirt, her ponytail loose and dishevelled. Her arms were wrapped tightly around her bare knees and her face was streaked with dust. Billy was sitting very still in the over-turned crate, his blue eyes jumping from Raven to Steve and back to Raven again. Steve sat hunched forward on the chair, elbows on knees, a dark fuzz of stubble over his chin, his face tired and drawn. Raven stood in front of the door, the jagged piece of glass still in his hand. His school shirt stuck to his skin in damp patches and there was blood on the hand that held the glass.

'Raven, put that down, you're going to hurt yourself,' Steve said quietly.

'Shut up,' Raven snapped.

'Oh, Raven,' Lotte said, her voice faltering. 'I thought you were my best friend, I really did! Why have you been lying about everything to me?'

'He's not well,' Steve said softly. 'It's not his fault. He was so devastated by the death of his mother—'

'Shut up!' Raven was shouting now.

With a whimper, Billy climbed out of the crate and ran over to his father's lap. Steve pulled Billy's face against his chest, hugging him tight. 'It's all right, Billy Boy,' he said. 'We're going home in a minute . . .'

Raven felt his hand tighten against the piece of glass and something warm and wet trickle between his fingers. He looked at Lotte. 'See, Billy's his son. I'm not.'

Steve shook his head slowly. 'You are both my sons. And I've always loved both of you equally. Why are you doing this? I never wanted social services to take you away, you know that.' His voice caught in his throat. 'But I couldn't cope with you, Raven. You were so angry and hostile. I just didn't know how to help you . . .'

Lotte looked at him beseechingly. 'Please unlock the door, Raven. Please let's just get out of here and go back to Steve's flat, and sit down and talk.' She sounded close to tears.

Raven looked from Steve to Lotte. He seemed to be breathing very fast and his cheeks were burning. 'Turn the camera on,' he said to Lotte.

She looked up at him from her crouching position against the wall, her eyes wide. 'What for?' she demanded, her voice suddenly angry again. 'The whole thing was just a lie!'

'Not a lie,' Raven said slowly, his eyes boring into hers. 'Not a lie! It can be real if you want it to be!' He swung round angrily to Steve. 'Take it back!' he shouted. 'Go on, admit that you killed my mum! Tell her you're not my father!'

'Why?' Steve asked, his face ashen. 'Why, Raven? How would that make it better?'

'It's the truth!'

'No, Raven, it's not,' Steve said. 'It's a story you invented in your mind to make yourself feel better. You wanted it to be true so badly, you ended up believing it.'

'I hate you!'

'I know, I know you do, Raven, but it's not because I killed Mum, is it? You think I let you down by allowing them to take you away. And maybe you're right, son. Maybe you're right.'

There was a silence. Raven stared at him. His hand throbbed and it hurt to breathe. Lotte rocked gently back and forth on her heels and Billy whimpered into Steve's shirt.

Suddenly Raven lunged forward, grabbed Billy by the arm and pulled him off Steve's lap. Steve made a grab for the little boy, but as Raven lifted the piece of glass to Billy's throat, he shrank back into his seat. Grasping Billy, Raven walked backwards to stand in front of the door.

Billy burst into noisy tears. 'I'll hurt him,' Raven warned Steve.

'Raven,' Lotte let out a sob. 'He's your brother!'

'He's not my brother!' Raven shouted at her.

Lotte got up onto her knees. 'Look at him!' she implored him. 'He looks just like you! You've both got the same brown hair and blue eyes! Of course he's your brother! He's only little and you're terrifying him!'

'Shut up!'

Billy tugged away from Raven, the sleeve of his sweatshirt in his mouth, wailing loudly.

Steve's breathing was laboured and his eyes were bulging.

'You're worse than Kyle and Brett!' Lotte suddenly shouted, her eyes flashing. 'You're scaring a small child. You're an even bigger bully than the ones at school!'

Raven glared at her, the blood throbbing in his cheeks. 'I'm not a bully,' he said slowly. 'I was never going to hurt him – I love him – I never wanted to hurt anybody.' His voice caught in his throat and he felt his eyes fill with tears. He let go of Billy, who stumbled back and then turned and ran into Steve's arms. Raven swayed. He felt dizzy suddenly. 'It wasn't meant to be like this' – his voice came out unevenly – 'I didn't mean to—'

'Just put down that piece of glass and unlock the door,' Steve said quietly. 'And it can all stop here.'

Raven tightened his hand against the jagged edge.

'Raven, your hand is bleeding,' Lotte said with a muffled sob. 'Please put the glass down, please!'

Raven's jaw ached. He looked at Steve. 'Just tell me the truth,' he said from between clenched teeth.

'The truth is that your mum slipped on the balcony and fell three storeys to her death,' Steve said. 'The truth is, we were all devastated by her loss. The truth is, the drink finally got to me and I had to go into rehab and you and Billy were taken into care. But when I came out of rehab and you and Billy came home, you were so angry with me you ran away, and I couldn't cope so social services took you into care again. The truth is that I love you but I just don't know how to help you any more.'

'You missed out one part,' Raven said.

Steve looked at him over Billy's cropped head, his blue eyes imploring. 'Which part, Raven?'

'This part,' Raven said, his throat tightening. 'The ending.'

'OK,' Steve said quickly, shakily. 'The ending is that Raven forgives his dad for falling apart. The ending is that Raven starts visiting his dad and brother for the weekends, and they all start spending time as a family

again.' He gave a small, hopeful smile. 'That's the
ending.'

Raven shook his head. 'No,' he said. 'The end is that
the real killer must die. That's the only proper ending.'

Steve's eyes widened in horror. 'No . . .' he whispered.
'Nobody needs to die.'

Raven stepped back. The glass made a clattering
sound as it fell from his hand to the floor. Steve got up.
Raven turned, unlocked the door and ran.

He took the steps three at a time, his feet clattering up
the threadbare staircase to the top of the house. In the
loft he skidded to a dizzying halt, looking around wildly.
Weak evening light fell through the skylights, casting a
bluish tinge over the dusty floor. There were two of them
on either side of the room. Pressing his forearms against
one, he heaved his full weight against it but it didn't
budge. He could hear Lotte's feet pounding up from the
floor below. 'Raven, wait! I want to talk to you! Wait for
me!' He tried the other skylight. Also stuck. By now he
could hear Lotte's panting, sobbing breath. He shut his
eyes and kicked the bottom of the pane as hard as he
could. There was a sound of breaking glass. A shout from
the staircase. He kicked the jagged bits away from the
bottom of the window and lifted one leg over the sill,
then the other. Something tore at his shirt. There was a

sharp pain in his side. As he clung to the bottom edge of the skylight, his head and shoulders still inside the room, his feet scrabbled against the slate tiles for a hold. Then his toes met the curved edge of the gutter along the front of the roof and he lowered his weight onto the balls of his feet. His knuckles were white against the edge of the skylight but he forced himself to move, one foot at a time, sidestepping away from it, across the roof. The skylight was suddenly replaced by cold, black slate tiles and he found himself gripping at their thin edges, his fingers white and shaking, his hands cramping with the effort as he clung like a limpet to the side of the roof. The wind tugged at his shirt-tails, ruffling his hair. He was painfully aware of the three-storey drop to the street below. Only his fingers and the balls of his feet were keeping him from plunging backwards into the void. He was aware too that he would not be able to cling on for ever. Eventually his muscles would give up. And he would have no choice but to let go. He noticed a flat bit between the two peaked skylights. He kept his eyes glued to it. Only another four steps to go.

When he reached it, his arms were shaking so much he could barely pull himself up. On his knees, the weight finally off his hands and feet, he slid himself round and looked down. The street, the cars, even the tops of the lit lampposts were way, way beneath him. It looked like a toy street, with miniature paving stones and a let's-pretend postbox on the corner. He stared down, hypnotized. What would it be like to fall all that way? Would you scream? Would you have time to shut your eyes before you hit the ground? And when you landed, you would look like a crumpled thing – not real, kind of like a rag doll in clothes, and one of your shoes would have fallen off and you wouldn't move at all . . .

Sometime later, much later, he heard the rusty squeak of a window opening nearby. Raven held his breath. There was a scrabbling, a panting noise. He tensed, poised, ready to move. Then came a voice he recognized.

'Raven, don't move,' Dan said. 'You're going to be OK. Remember what I said at the slide? I will never let you fall.'

Raven let his eyes flick over to the window. Dan was carefully climbing out, edging slowly towards him along the narrow parapet.

'Don't come any nearer,' Raven said. 'I'll jump, I swear I will.'

'I believe you,' Dan replied. He pulled himself up onto the roof, his legs dangling down. 'Bit chilly here, isn't it?'

Raven turned his head away and looked back down at the lamplit street below. A huddle of people now stood on the pavement, gazing up. A fire engine had pulled up on the street corner, its blue lights flashing silently. Raven lowered his feet over the edge of the roof and shuffled forwards.

'This is how your mother died, isn't it?' Dan said quietly. 'By falling.'

Raven hesitated, then nodded.

'What a terrible accident.'

Raven said nothing. He looked up at the evening sky.

'It *was* an accident,' Dan said quietly.

Raven turned his head to look at him. Dan was sitting there, inches away from the roof edge. In the fading evening light his face looked placid, eerie almost in its calmness, his expression no different to the one he had when they all sat playing Monopoly. The back of his shirt puffed out in the breeze.

'It was an argument, Raven. It was just an argument. People have arguments all the time.'

Raven could feel the thud of blood in his temples. It was difficult to breathe.

'It was only a push. You didn't think she would lose her footing like that. You didn't think the railing would break and she would fall.'

Raven leaned forward slowly, carefully, towards the void. The wind tugged at his shirt-tails.

'You think that if you pushed your mum, in anger, while you were having an argument, you killed her,' Dan said, his voice gathering speed. 'But it was just an argument. People have arguments all the time.'

Raven could feel himself sway.

'You think that you deserve to die for what you did,' Dan went on. 'But you're wrong. Very wrong. It was an accident. A complete and utter accident. Everyone's always known that, except you. I want you to take my hand.'

The tears in Raven's eyes kaleidoscoped the lights from the street below. 'I want to tell her I'm sorry,' he whispered.

'I'm sure she knows,' Dan replied. He still sounded calm but there was a slight tremor to his voice. 'The last thing she would ever have wanted was for you to die too.'

'I didn't think she would fall!' A sob escaped him now.

'Of course you didn't,' Dan said. He leaned across the roof, stretching out his arm.

Raven stared at him, breathing hard. 'Make her come back.'

Dan looked at him gently. 'You know I can't do that, Raven.'

Tears coursed down his cheeks. 'Please!'

'We love you, Raven. Ella adores you. She couldn't cope if anything happened to you. And Lotte's downstairs, waiting for you. I think she really cares about you. Even now that she knows the truth, she wants to make sure you're all right, she wants to talk to you. Please come back to all of us. It's what your mum would have wanted more than anything in the world. For you to be safe. For you to be happy.'

Raven teetered for a moment on the edge of the rooftop, at the brink of the night sky. Then he reached back and took Dan's hand.